New TOEIC Listening Script

*install ① have sth. installed = We've had a second phone line installed.
安裝 ② install sb. as sth.= She was installed as the first Chancellor of the university. 擔任這所大學第一位校長

PART 1

③ install oneself: After arriving the store, Ashely installed herself behind the table. 于

1. (A)
   (A) The man is moving some boxes in a warehouse. 安裝 遮孝積
   (B) The man is installing a window in a factory.
   (C) The man is reading a newspaper in an airport.
   (D) The man is watching a movie in a theater. 電影院

*be full of O. 充滿 全神貫注的: He was full of his own importance. 他只想著自己

2. (D)
   (A) The worker is driving a truck.
   (B) The beach is full of trash. v.挖: They were
   n.鏟子
   挖土機
   (C) The shovel is on the shelf. shoveling coal into the
   (D) The helmet is on the grass. cart. 把煤挖進推車裡
   v.塞,挖

v.塞: He shovelled the food into his mouth.

3. (B)
   (A) The lawyer is taking some notes.
   (B) The doctor is giving the man a shot. 給這個男生一針
   (C) The chef is greeting a customer. (幫他他針)
   erase
   (D) The teacher is erasing the blackboard. 和客人打招呼

*file ①. keep
   hold a file on sth./sb. The company keeps
   personal files on all its employees 員工個資在檔
4. (B)
   (A) The man is using a computer.
   (B) The man is looking in a file cabinet. 檔案櫃
   (C) The man is opening a door. ② on file 在檔
   (D) The man is sitting on the floor. We have all your
   details on file.

It's a demonstration of his love.
   他愛意的展現
5. (A)
   (A) Some people are working in a kitchen.
   (B) Some people are working in a bank. 廣示
   demonstrate 證明
   (C) Some people are watching a demonstration.
   (D) Some people are participating in a survey.
   participate v.

6. (D)
   (A) Some people are shopping in the market.
   queue up 排隊
   (B) Some people are lined up at an airport.
   board n.板子 v.登車.機.船.住
   (C) Some people are boarding a bus.
   board house
   (D) Some people are waiting for a train.

→ He was boarded out with foster parents. 養父母 新的家庭
→ board certified 取得專業証照的 → board exam 專業證照考試 (醫護類)

PART 2

建築檢查員
see 人　應該要到這程？

7. (A) What time is the <u>building inspector</u> supposed to be here?　inspect v. 檢查 查閱　introspect v. 內省
   (A) Sometime in the afternoon.
   (B) Yes, but they usually do.　inspection n. ～ ～　inside
   (C) The new subway station.　introspection n. ～
   新的地鐵站　戎孕　大眾. (商品名稱)

8. (A) Excuse me, I'm <u>looking for</u> Gina's Hot Sauce.
   (A) That item is out of stock. 那樣商品已經沒有庫存 (out of stock) →賣完了
   (B) No, thanks.　　　←→ in stock 有庫存
   (C) I don't think she's here. 戎不覺得她在這裡　The new cold and flu medicine
   正鉤, 倉庫是開著的, 對嗎？　was so popular that a stockout occured.

9. (C) The warehouse is open, isn't it?　因市場需求太大而無法正常候貨
   (A) There should be plenty of room.
   (B) Mostly boxes of old files.　　應該有很多房間
   (C) Yes, but I'm just <u>about to</u> lock it up.　大部分是舊檔案的盒子
   戎正要鎖起來。

10. (A) When will the new line of products be <u>released</u>? 新商品線何時會提出？
    release　(A) Most likely in late October.
    v. 釋放. 放鬆　(B) Yes, an <u>updated version</u>.　be about to　be ready to
    諒免. 放棄. 發行　(C) It's one of my favorite cities. 那將 (very soon)　準備 (likely to happen)
    更新的版本 (說法)

11. (B) Where is the nearest post office? 最近的郵局在那裡
    (A) No, you didn't get any messages. 沒辦法告訴你, 戎不是這附近的人
    (B) Couldn't tell you. <u>I'm not from around here</u>.
    (C) During my break. 在戎休假期間　*mind ①用於否定和疑問句中有意
    你介不介意明天在會議室B程開會？　②注意：Mind the wet paint.

12. (B) Would you <u>mind</u> holding your meeting in conference room B tomorrow?
    (A) I thought he retired last year.　③照料：He can mind your
    (B) Sure, that works for me. 戎可以唷！　shop for you.
    (C) Yes, they're new workers. 他們是新的工作者　幫你看店
    intern v. 拘留. 軟禁

13. (B) How long will the <u>interns</u> work in the office?
    (A) Dave and Steve. n. 實習生　→ The contract between the two
    (B) Only an hour or two.　companies will expire at the end of
    (C) You're welcome.　expire v. 到期　the year.
    你的證照不是這個月到期嗎？　到期　My membership in the club has
    14. (C) Isn't your driver's license <u>due to expire</u> this month?　expired.
    (A) She's an experienced driver. 有經驗的駕駛　That reminds me!
    (B) It was much longer than that. 比那個還長　倒是提醒了戎
    (C) Oh, thanks for reminding me.　Don't remind me! 別跟戎提
    謝謝提醒

15. (A) Should we be seated in a circle or set up in rows? 按照圓圈坐還是坐成一排排?

(A) Aren't we going to be watching a video?　*row n. 一列. 一排 in a row

(B) Just some coffee, please. 根據尺寸大小安排的

(C) No. Arrange them according to size. → to go for a row 去划船

according adj. 相應的 You need to make an according /raʊ/ n. 吵架 v. 爭吵. 吵鬧

decision. 做個相應的決定

16. (C) Why don't you try re-installing the software? → Helen rowed with her boyfriend

取決於 (A) Depends on when the manager arrives. about a mere trifle. 瑣事. 小事

(B) That's the number for technical support. /tɪ/

(C) I already tried that. 技術支持部的號碼 因為一件小事和男友吵架

我不建議停在地下室車庫裡 *supply

17. (B) I don't recommend parking in the underground garage. n. 補給品. 生活費 supplies

(A) On the top shelf in the supply closet. 儲物櫃最上層 v. 供應

(B) I've heard that before. 我有聽過這個說法 Cotton is the staple

(C) 50 copies, stapled please. staple v. 釘 of the area.

這趟旅行應該不會超過20分鐘. 對嗎? /e/ n. 訂書針. 釘, 主要商品

18. (A) The trip shouldn't take longer than 20 minutes, should it? stapler 釘書機

(A) No. It should be fairly quick. 頗快

(B) Yes, it was quite informative. adj. 增廣見聞的 information age 資訊時代

(C) No, you can walk there. 'analyst 情報分析員

我要如何保留(預約)首映會的位置? /ˈænl̩ɪst/ 延伸義

19. (B) How can I reserve seats for the premiere of the film? property 房地產 → 財產. 資產

(A) Right. That was yesterday. /prɪˈmɪr/ 首映

(B) Go to our website. (props) riches rich → 財物. 財寶

(C) It went very well. 進行得非常順利 官饒的

那些財產名單更新了嗎? → 財產. 房產. 道具 wealth 幸福 → 財富

20. (C) Have those property listings been updated yet?

(A) I'll have some, thanks. fortune 幸運女神 → 財富

(B) They're actually undersized. 他們其實太小了

(C) We finished doing that before lunch. 午餐之前會做完

你覺得他會給我們更多時間做預算報告嗎?

21. (A) Do you think Ms. Brown will give us more time on the budget reports?

(A) The deadline is non-negotiable. 截止期限是沒得商量的

(B) That makes it easier to make a decision. 做決定更簡單了

(C) Some took a bit longer. 有些花比較長的時間

你有任何推薦的義大利菜嗎?

22. (B) Do you have any recommendations for Italian food? *approval

(A) I received her supervisor's approval. 我收到她主管的同意書 n. 批准. 認可

(B) Giuseppe's on Elm Street is fantastic. 同意

(C) A four-mile run. 跑四哩　超棒的

GO ON TO THE NEXT PAGE

23. (A) Please fill out this questionnaire before tomorrow's final interview.
   (A) I'll be sure to do that.   明天最後面試之前請填好這個問卷
   (B) It's a new survey.
   (C) I saw him on the subway.

① 填寫
carry out / conduct a 'survey n' 研究 ② 房子稽查
③ 勘測 (為了做地圖)

② 長胖: Sam has really filled out, hasn't he?

24. (A) Mr. Levin usually leaves the office at 5:30, doesn't he?
   (A) Five nights a week.   一週有5天都是這樣   他通常都5:30離開辦公室,
   (B) No. I ordered the fish.   是嗎?
   (C) Traffic was surprisingly light today.   今天交通很輕 (沒有塞車)

和原本不一樣而導致的吃驚   (通常是會塞的)

25. (B) Where did the board of directors decide to build a new office tower?
   (A) Sales were average.   董事會決定要在哪裡蓋新辦公樓?
   (B) In Chicago.
   (C) October 1st.   銷售很平均

Not surprisingly, everyone got drunk at the wedding.

樣行處~我們要選新的油漆顏色

26. (C) We're choosing new paint colors for the reception area.   不出所料, 婚禮每個人
   (A) Where's the waiter?   都喝醉了
   (B) A new director was selected.   新的指導員 (主任, 處長, 指導員, 經理)
   (C) Coleman's Home & Hardware has a great selection.   有很好的系列 (商品)

為何這些操作指南只有中文的?

27. (B) Why are these instructions only in Chinese?   selection
   (A) Thanks for coming in early today.   謝謝你今天早點進來   1. 選擇, 選拔 2. 選出來的人/物
   (B) I've asked Jill to have them translated.
   (C) We have enough copies for everyone?   bring

我有要叫川把它們翻譯一下   translate (帶到別處)   selection process / procedure / policy   選拔 流程 政策

28. (C) Which event space would you like to use?   v. 將譯, 解譯, 說明
   (A) Let's try for mid September.
   (B) We should hire her.   我們應該聘請她   4. make a selection 精心選擇
   (C) I like the first one you showed me.   → It's worth taking the time to make a careful selection.

我喜歡你給我看的第一個   值得花時間用心挑選

29. (C) Who's recording the radio advertisement scripts?
   (A) We're open 24 hours.   *script
   (B) At 7 o'clock on Monday.   劇本, 字跡, 考卷
   (C) That decision hasn't been made.   she had a large pile of scripts to mark. 有一疊考卷要改

你有寄出開幕式的邀請函了嗎?

30. (A) Have you sent out the invitations for the grand opening?   宏偉的, 盛大的開幕
   (A) I didn't get a guest list.
   (B) I'm planning on going too.   我正要去慶要去
   (C) Outside of the conference center.

31. (B) When will the car come to take us to the conference? 車何時會來接我們去開會
    (A) In front of the hotel. 在飯店前面
    (B) The driver will call when he's arrived. 駕駛到的時候會打電話
    (C) Because it's too far to walk. 太遠了以至於走不到

太~以至於不能~
too~ to do sth. *too可以當adv.放在 adj. many / adv. much few 之前
→ They are too busy.
→ The sight of suffering was too much for him. 難過的眼神他承受不了

PART 3

Questions 32 through 34 refer to the following conversation.

特別(特製)訂單怎麼了？

W : Chad, what's going on with the special order of T-shirts for the San Diego Marathon? The event organizers are coming to pick them up this afternoon. 今下午來拿 ※跑 馬拉松

M : Had a bit of a setback, Lois. When I turned on the screen printing press this morning, I noticed the automatic squeegee had not been cleaned properly. So I had to take it apart and clean it before moving forward. 橡膠滾軸沒有恰當的清理 (不乾淨) 要拆開重組 檢查
有一點挫折/失敗(遇到了某問題)

W : Oh, who was the last person to use the press? 誰是最後用印表機的人？

M : I don't know. But I took care of it. No big deal. Cost me an hour, but I'll have the T-shirts ready this afternoon. 我會處理這事的
雖然花我一個小時 但我今天下午會把衣服準備好

32. (A) Where do the speakers most likely work?
    (A) At a custom print shop. 客製印刷店
    (B) At a construction site. 建設地(蓋房子的地方)
    (C) In a bakery.
    (D) In an appliance store. 電器行 *appliance

33. (D) What problem does the man mention? 器具.設備.應用 ≒ equipment (依照工作性質所需的工具)
運送延遲 (A) A shipment was delayed. toaster oven microwave 都是
訂單取消 (B) An order was cancelled.
員工遲到 (C) An employee was late to work.
機器沒有正確清理 (D) A machine was not cleaned properly.
hammer tape measure 捲尺

34. (B) What will happen this afternoon?
    (A) A business will close. 店家關門
    (B) An order will be completed. 訂單完成
    (C) A repair person will arrive. 維修人員到達
    (D) An event will be set up. 活動安排起來(準備好)

Questions 35 through 37 refer to the following conversation.

我又來看老虎隊比賽的, 我把我所有的現金花在點心和飲料和紀念品上

M : Hey, I was here for the Tigers game, but I spent all my cash on snacks and drinks and souvenirs. Do you accept credit cards? 你們收信用卡嗎？

GO ON TO THE NEXT PAGE.

W : I can't process a credit card here at the exit, but you have two options. There's an ATM on the third level of the parking garage, right as you exit the concourse of the stadium. Or...if you have Internet access on your phone, you can pay online.

M : That's a great idea. I'll pay online. And, what's the website address that I should use?

W : The address is printed on the back of your parking ticket.

M : And then what?

W : Once you've paid the fee online, you'll get a confirmation code emailed to you. Give me the code and I'll process your exit.

35. (A) Where are the speakers?
   (A) In a parking garage.
   (B) In a restaurant.
   (C) In a movie theater.
   (D) In a bank.

36. (C) What does the man decide to do?
   (A) Withdraw money from a cash machine.
   (B) Call a customer service number.
   (C) Make a payment online.
   (D) Return at a later time.

37. (A) What will be sent to the man?
   (A) A confirmation number.
   (B) A warranty offer.
   (C) An account statement.
   (D) A VIP membership card.

Questions 38 through 40 refer to the following conversation.

M : Tiffany, you're coordinating the orientation program for new hires, correct? I need to double-check with you about the new sales associate. You still want me to review the benefits package with him, right?

W : I do. He'll be starting on Wednesday morning, and I was hoping you could talk to him right after lunch that afternoon.

M : Mmm... That's what I thought. I scheduled another meeting with Serena on Wednesday at 1 P.M. Is there any way that I can meet with the new guy in the morning?

W : Well, he's going to be working the floor in housewares, and they generally have a tight schedule for new hires. Don't worry about it. I'll have Jeff cover for you.

M : Thanks, Tiffany. Sorry about that.

50

W : I know, Ted. It's just been rather hectic in accounting lately, and the report... The main sticking point is the estimated cost of computer equipment and upgrades for our new hires. Based on the number of new employees, we're going to be spending way more than usual. But it's hard to say exactly how much.

M : I get that. We have some flexibility for increasing our spending right now. We're all aware of the increase in staff, so... Let's see what the other managers can do about renegotiating our contract with Tacer Electronics. Hopefully, we can get a better deal.

47. (A) What does the man mean by, "So...the accounting expense proposal"?
    (A) He wants to know if a document is ready.
    (B) He wants to extend a deadline.
    (C) He wants to know if schedule has been changed.
    (D) He wants an explanation for a policy decision.

48. (B) What does the woman say about an expense estimate?
    (A) It has been misplaced.
    (B) It will be higher than expected.
    (C) It was already approved.
    (D) It contained some mistakes.

49. (A) What will the man discuss at a meeting?
    (A) Contracts with vendors.
    (B) Design modifications.
    (C) Accounting practices.
    (D) Candidates for a career promotion.

Questions 50 through 52 *refer to the following conversation.*

W : Gabe, all the news reports are saying the big snowstorm heading our way may disrupt bus and train service tomorrow, and I'm scheduled to open the store.

M : I know, Paola. Sounds like it's going to be a major storm, and most of our employees use public transportation. So, I'm thinking about closing the store tomorrow altogether, but want to keep an eye on the weather reports. I'll make a decision before closing tonight.

W : Let me know if you need help contacting the rest of the staff.

M : Will do. Thanks for your care and concern, Paola.

50. (D) What problem does the woman mention?
    (A) Parking in the area is limited.
    (B) The sales forecast is negative.
    (C) Customer complaints have increased.
    (D) Bad weather has been predicted.

GO ON TO THE NEXT PAGE.

53

51. (C) What does the man say he will decide this evening?

(A) When to launch a new sales promotion. 何時要推出新的銷售促銷方案

(B) When to meet with investors. 何時要跟投資者會面

(C) Whether the store will be closed. 店是否會關門

(D) Whether additional employees should be hired. 是否該雇用多的員工

女士說要幫男士什麼事?

52. (C) What does the woman offer to help the man with?

(A) Organizing a carpool. 安排共乘 *organize v. 組織. 安排

(B) Revising a work schedule. 檢視工作行程 revise v. 檢視

(C) Contacting employees. 聯絡員工 *organized adj. + person 有條理的人

(D) Opening the store. 開店 + desk / kitchen 井井有條

Questions 53 through 55 *refer to the following conversation.*

不好意思. 我看到一些陳列的頭掛式耳機, 想知道它們售價多少. 你可以幫我嗎?

W : Excuse me. I saw some headphones on display and I want to know how much they cost. Can you help me? 當然! 哪一組耳機呢?

M : Sure! Which pair of headphones is it?

它們聲音聽起來很好. 但是這副耳機沒有標票價

W : These red Sonic Blasters. They sound great. But this pair doesn't have a price tag.

M : Oh yeah. Those are nice. The price tag should be on the box. 標價應該在盒子上

W : Actually, the box isn't on the shelf. 事實上. 盒子沒有在架子上

M : That's strange. Anyway, I'll look up the price in our system. Give me a minute.

那就怪了. 反正我會進系統幫你查詢價格 *look up 查詢

53. (A) What does the woman ask the man about?

(A) The price of an item. 一個商品的價格 轉好

(B) The location of a store. 一個商店的地點 Inflation is coming down;

(C) The maker of a product. 商品製造商 unemployment is coming down;

(D) The availability of colors. 可選擇的顏色 things are definitely looking up!

54. (D) Why does the man say, "Those are nice"?

說服 (A) To convince a friend to buy headphones. 通膨減緩了.

(B) To suggest an alternative product. 建議送 失業減緩了

(C) To compliment a co-worker. 祝賀同事 別的商品 事情絕對會好轉的!

(D) To express agreement. 表達同意 *alternative adj. 替代的 可供選擇的

55. (B) What does the man say he will do? 類似的. 差不多的. 可相比的

(A) Find a comparable item. n. 供選擇的東西

(B) Check a price list. 查看價格表

(C) Print a receipt. 印收據 *compliment v. 讚美. 祝賀

(D) Provide a coupon code.

Questions 56 through 58 *refer to the following conversation.*

M : Yeah, hi. This is Bruce Wright. I ordered a vacuum cleaner from you guys three days ago. I paid for next day shipping and it hasn't arrived yet. The tracking number is HOV283. Would you mind letting me know what's happened to it?

W : Mr. Wright, thanks for calling. Okay, let me run that tracking number. Yes, my system indicates that a delivery was attempted yesterday at 301 North Elm Street in Berkeley. The driver reported no one home to accept delivery.

M : But, that's my home address! I specifically indicated an alternate delivery address. Why didn't the driver call me? My phone number is on the invoice.

W : You're right. It appears the vacuum cleaner was automatically sent to your billing address. I apologize for that. Let me confirm your information now so that I can reschedule the delivery. To compensate for the inconvenience, I'll have it sent priority, and refund the delivery fee to your credit card.

56. (C) Why is the man calling?
    (A) To schedule a repair.
    (B) To inquire about a bill.
    (C) To check the status of an order.
    (D) To provide an updated credit card number.

57. (A) What problem does the woman mention?
    (A) A product was sent to the wrong address.
    (B) A product is no longer available.
    (C) A deadline was missed.
    (D) A credit card payment was not received.

58. (B) What does the woman offer to do?
    (A) Speak with a supervisor.
    (B) Issue a refund.
    (C) Change a password.
    (D) Add a warranty.

Questions 59 through 61 *refer to the following conversation with three speakers.*

Woman US : Oh good, you're both here. We need to plan our strategy for next month's travel fair in Chicago. So, what should we focus on first?

Woman UK : Well, our travel agency only has a booth at the fair for two days. That's not a lot of time to make a big impression.

M : I think we should develop a brochure that highlights some of our most popular tours and destinations. Can you put that together with me, Sophia?

GO ON TO THE NEXT PAGE.

55

Woman UK : Yes, but we're under a tight deadline. It has to be sent to the printers by next week 為了 in order to have it in time for the travel fair. 但是我們離截止日期有點緊

必須先送至印刷場下週之前

以求得及趕上下週的旅行展

59. (D) What is the conversation mainly about?
   (A) Finding a guest speaker for a convention. (A)為大會找來客座講者
   (B) Creating an employee handbook. (B)創作員工手冊
   (C) Organizing a training session. (C)組織訓練活動
   (D) Preparing for a business exposition. (D)準備商務展覽會
                                      EX

60. (B) What does the man suggest doing?
   (A) Reserving more time 保留更多時間 → ①展覽會 Expo
   (B) Revising a timetable. 檢查時刻表
   (C) Sending out invitations. ②說明·闡述 This is a clear exposition
        寄出邀請函   of the theory of evolution.
   (D) Making a brochure.
        做手冊   這是對進化論的清晰闡述

61. (C) What does Sophia say she is concerned about?
   (A) A canceled reservation. 一個取消的預訂 Sophia 說她擔心什麼
   (B) An unconfirmed meeting. 一個未確認的會議
   (C) An approaching deadline.
        一個快接近的期限
   (D) An incorrect report.
   approach v. 接近,靠近 一個不正確的報告

Questions 62 through 64 *refer to the following conversation and floor plan.*

in particular 特別地,尤其

M : Good morning, welcome to Ruby's Books and Café. Can I help you find something in
   particular? adj. 特殊的·特定的·特別的 社群媒體的崛起

W : Yes, I need a copy of a book called *The Rise of Social Media*. My friends and I are starting
   a book club next month. I've heard it's a fascinating read and a good title for discussion.
   難免地(不意外) 社群媒體是現在的熱話題 迷的·極好的 討論的好題材

M : No doubt. Social media is a hot topic these days. Anyway, you can find it on the first floor
   on the back wall of the store next to the café. Almost all our books are arranged by author.
   Can I interest you in a cup of coffee in our café?

W : No, thanks, but I think I'll browse for a little while.
        I'm just browsing. 隨便看看

你會在一樓咖啡店旁邊商店的後牆
找到. 我們所有的書幾乎都是用
作者排序的. 我可以招攬你一杯我們
店裡的咖啡嗎?

62. (A) Who most likely is the man?
   (A) A sales clerk. 售貨員 *interest
   (B) A baker. 麵包師 v. ①It may interest
   (C) An author. 作者   you to learn / know / hear.
   (D) A teacher. 老師   ②招攬 hear about 知道

* series 系列. 一組
a series of attacks
                measures

63. (A) What does the woman say she heard about the book?
   (A) It will provide opportunities for discussion. 提供討論的機會 一連串攻擊
   (B) It is the first book in a series. 是這系列中的第一本   一系列
   (C) It has been a best-seller for many months. 是好幾個月以來賣最好的 措施
   (D) It was written by an associate. 是同事/同行寫的

56

64. (C) Look at the graphic. In which section is the book that the woman is looking for?

看這個圖表、這個女人要找的書在哪一區?

(A) Travel.
(B) Reference. → 參考文獻
(C) Non-fiction. → 紀實文學 (傳記, 如何蓋學校)
(D) Young Adult.

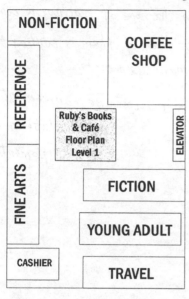

保養, 煮菜 etc... 把實際情況寫下來
不是杜撰的

fiction n.小說, 虛構, 捏造
fine arts 藝術 (畫, 建築, 詩歌, 音樂)
reference 文獻, 提及

→ get sth. down to a fine art
(D) 將某事做得盡善盡美
→ She's got the business of buying birthday presents down to a fine art.
她對於買生日禮物非常在行

Questions 65 through 67 refer to the following conversation and review.

CLM 的新刊物已經出版了, 我想你們已經看過這篇 "當地最棒餐廳" 的文章了吧

W : The new issue of *Franklin County Living Magazine* is out. I guess you've seen the article with the list of the best local restaurants? The article gave our restaurant five stars in the category of customer service. As the general manager, you must be proud. 身為總經理, 你該感到驕傲

M : Well, I think the article confirms it was a good decision to hire more staff this spring. It shows that customers appreciate attentive service.

這篇文章確定了今年春天我們要僱用更多的員工, 都喜歡殷勤的服務 (仔細的服務, 人手要夠)

W : True, but I'm disappointed that some of our ratings weren't better. I'm not surprised that we scored low in the menu options category, but I am surprised by this one, where we received only two stars. We'll have to address that area of concern as soon as possible.

的確, 但我對於有些評分沒能更好有些失望
在菜單選擇上, 分數低我不意外, 但我很驚訝這個
只有收到2顆星, 我們要點出這部分的問題

M : Yes, it may be a good idea to meet with the owners. We have no control over that. <u>They may be willing to make a few compromises.</u> 妥協(讓)

對, 跟老闆談是個好主意, 這不是我們能自己決定的, 他們(老闆)可能願意做些妥協

65. (B) Who is the man?
(A) An editor. 編輯
(B) A manager.
(C) A financial consultant. 財務顧問
(D) A food critic. 食物評論家

GO ON TO THE NEXT PAGE.

57

66. (D) Look at the graphic. What area does the woman want the restaurant to improve in?
    (A) Customer service. 客服
    (B) Menu options. 菜單選擇
    (C) Atmosphere. 氣氛
    (D) Prices and value. 價格和價值

*compromise
n. 妥協
→ Both sides have agreed to meet, in the hope of reaching a compromise.
→ Neither of them is willing to make compromises.
a compromise agreement 協議
solution 解決方式
settlement 和解

Silk Road Restaurant Rating

Atmosphere
★★★★

Prices and value
★★

Customer service
★★★★★

Menu options
★★★

price - performance
cost - performance
ratio
↳壞比 CP值
=性能÷價格

67. (A) What does the man mean when he says, "They may be willing to make a few compromises"? 老闆可能同意降低價格
    (A) The owners may agree to lower prices. 老闆可能希望拓展生意
    (B) The owners may wish to expand the business.
    (C) The critics may welcome another visit. 評論家可以再去吃一次
    (D) The staff may appreciate the time off. 員工很感激休假

/ˈzɛbrəˌtɔri/ 實驗室 菜廠

Questions 68 through 70 refer to the following conversation and picture.

laboratory

W : In this afternoon's lab training session, we'll discuss monitoring the barometer batteries. If the power's too low, we won't know the exact pressure within the lab. This is incredibly important when conducting research. 執行研究 conduct undertake carry out 超級重要 監督氣壓表的電池

M : Do the barometers use an independent power source or run on batteries?
氣壓計有自己的獨立供電還是是用電池的呢? 你需要仔細地監督電池

W : Batteries. And that's the most important point. You'll need to monitor the battery closely; always check the display screen. 一直查看顯示螢幕 電量等級會被陳列(顯示)

M : When do the batteries need to be replaced? 電池何時需要被更換 在單位上(那個東西上)
如同你們受訓手冊裡寫的 →新兵、練生

W : As described in your trainee manual, the battery power levels will be displayed on the unit. Replace batteries when they reach 25 percent. We don't want to swap them out any earlier than we have to, but we'll lose valuable time and data if the barometers need to be reset.
25%時要換電池，我們不想太早把電池換出來、但若氣壓計需要重新設定會失去保貴的時間(太早 太晚 都不可以)

58

68. (C) What event is taking place? 什麼活動正在舉行　＊補充講電話　開門見山
    (A) A sales meeting. 銷售會議
    (B) An award ceremony. 授獎典禮　→ I'm interested in your
    (C) A training session.　new software.
    (D) A weather forecast. 訓練活動　Can you give me a quote?
        氣象預報　/kwot/
        = an estimate

69. (D) What does the man ask about? 男的在問
    (A) Additional safety procedures. 多的安全流程
    (B) Different lab facilities. 不同的實驗室設備 → I'm calling to check my
    (C) Experiment results. 實驗結果　order status.
    (D) Alternative power sources.
        不同的電力來源 → I was refered to you by ～

70. (C) Look at the graphic. According to the woman, how many bars will be displayed
    when the battery should be replaced? 我是誰介紹來的
    (A) Three bars. 當電池需要被更換時, 會剩下幾個 bar
    (B) Two bars.　n. 條.棒
    (C) One bar.
    (D) Zero bars. → Sorry, I'm having a little
        trouble hearing.
        Could you slow down a little?
        I didn't quite catch that.
        Could you repeat it, please.

| 0-25% | 26-50% WEAK | 51-75% ACCEPTABLE | 76-100% IDEAL |

＊ 川普的女兒說 Those who say it can not be done, should not interrupt
        those doing it.
   類似的句子: If you can do it, go for it.
        If you can't do it, then don't criticize it.
        : Do not impose on others what yourself do not desire.
            (己所不欲, 勿施於人)
        : Those who can make big changes don't go with the
        usual way common people take.
        (成大事者, 不謀於眾)

GO ON TO THE NEXT PAGE

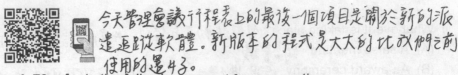

PART 4

今天管理會議行程表上的最後一個項目是關於新的派遣追蹤軟體。新版本的程式是大大的比我們之前使用的還好。

Questions 71 through 73 *refer to the following excerpt from a meeting.*

n. 議程.日常工作事項　　　　v. 涉及.關心.關於　n. 雙車過渡期

The last item on the agenda for this managers' meeting concerns the transition to our
new dispatch tracking software. The new version of the program is significantly more
sophisticated than the one we've been using. This software will allow us to track every
single driver in our fleet, regardless of where they are or where they're heading. This
will benefit our customers by reducing the time it takes to book a taxi. We will start
training dispatchers on using the software next week. Ms. Leslie Eastman, a trainer
from the software company, will be on site all week to do the training.

v. 派遣
精通的(下)
的一位經理
是要使我們的顧客受惠.在較少的時間訂計程車　我們將會
開始訓練調度員使用這個軟體
他整週都將會在現場做訓練

這個軟體使我們有能追蹤車隊裡頭
不論他們在哪裡或是他們要去哪裡

公司的什麼事情將會改變

71. (B) According to the speaker, what will be changing at the company?
　　(A) How drivers' hours are scheduled. 司機的上班時數如何安排
　　(B) How drivers are tracked. 司機如何被追蹤
　　　　bv. vpp.
　　(C) How customer complaints are handled. 客戶抱怨如何被處理
　　(D) How reservations are submitted. 預約如何被呈交

72. (A) What will the company be able to do for customers? ＊sophisticated
　　(A) Reduce wait times. 減少等待時間　　　　　wise
　　(B) Extend service routes. 增加服務路線　D. Consumers are getting more
　　(C) Lower prices. 降低價格　　　　　sophisticated and demanding.
　　(D) Offer more products. 提供更的商品　　越來越懂.要求越來越多

73. (D) What will Ms. Eastman be doing?　　② She is elegant and sophisticated.
　　(A) Conducting a survey. 執行一個調查　　優雅又得體
　　(B) Inspecting vehicles. inspect 檢查 sth. closely
　　(C) Testing equipment. ↘ look　　carefully 仔細檢查
　　(D) Training employees. ↘測試設備　thoroughly
　　　　　　↘訓練員工　1030上

Questions 74 through 76 *refer to the following telephone message.*

我打來問一個問題　　　　　　我搭sheffield線

Hi, my name is Jeff Sweeney and I'm calling about an issue... I ride the Sheffield Line
from Halston Street station every morning around 7:00, headed downtown. This
morning, I along with dozens of other people, waited over an hour on the platform
before giving up and taking a taxi. There was no announcement or explanation for the
delay, and no agent working the station. Then, I checked your company's website for
news about delays, but there wasn't any current information posted. So... I decided to

往市中心的方向
我和幾10名其他的人等了超過一個小時.
在我放棄等待或搭計程車之前
站內也沒有工作人員
延遲的事.但是沒有張貼任何目前消息
沒有通知或解釋任何延遲
那我也去看了你們公司的網站關於

所以我決定撥打熱線

call this information hotline. Can you tell me if there's been a change to the Sheffield

Line train schedule? I need to know today, please, before my workday ends. My

phone number is 727-0987. Thanks. 今天我下班之前需要知道答案

他打給什麼樣的行業
74. (C) What business is the speaker calling?　　　　　* industrial
　　　(A) A dentist's office. 牙醫辦公室 (牙醫診所)
　　　(B) A shoe repair shop. 修鞋店　　　+ waste　工業廢棄物
　　　(C) A transportation service. 交通服務　　+ unrest　工人動亂
　　　(D) A travel agency. 旅行社　　　　　+ dispute　勞資糾紛

　　　　　　　　　　　　　　　　　　　　　+ espionage 商業間諜活動
75. (D) Why did the speaker take a taxi?　　　　　　　/ɛspɪənaʒ/
　　　(A) He was concerned about parking. 擔心停車問題
　　　(B) He was late for a dinner date. 晚餐約會遲到
　　　(C) His car broke down. 車壞了 → break down
　　　(D) His train never arrived. 火車不來
　　　　　　　　　　　　　　因機械.電力同障
　　　　　　　　　　　　　　停止運轉.失敗.失效.崩潰.瓦解.垮
76. (B) What would the speaker like to know?
　　　(A) How to get to an event. 如何到達活動地點　　* hotline 最早是
　　　(B) Whether a schedule has changed. 行程是否有變動　白宮.克里姆林宮之間
　　　(C) When a new service will begin. 當新服務開始　　俄美蘇聯絡緊急狀況
　　　(D) How much a membership will cost.
　　　　　　　　　　　　　　會員要花多少錢

Questions 77 through 79 refer to the following telephone message.

　　　　　　　不動產　　　　有個新的倉庫空間剛剛釋出我們還沒列上去
Hi, this is Jennifer from Storch Real Estate. There's a new warehouse space that just
　　　　　　　　　　　　　　我想你會很喜歡
came on the market that we haven't listed yet. I think you'd really like it. It's in the
倉庫位在工業區　　　　　如你所想要的　　　唯一的問題可能是租金
heart of the industrial district, just like you wanted. The only problem may be that the
比你一開始的範圍高一點點　　　　但是倉庫空間比我們看過的其他間大多了
rent is higher than your initial range, but the warehouse space is much larger than the
　　　　你提到過要拓展你的生意　　　　　　所以我知道這會
others we've seen. You mentioned expanding your business, and so I knew it would
是你有興趣的
be something you'd be interested in. Now, I'll need you to let me know as soon as you

get this message if you want to see it. I won't list the property until I hear back from

you, but I can't hold it for too long. 我不會把這個物件放上去直到你回覆我, 但我
　　　　　　　　　　* initial adj. 起初的　沒辦法保留太久
77. (A) Who most likely is the speaker?
　　　(A) A real estate agent.　　* hear + sth. 聲音自然進入耳朵, 沒有刻意
　　　(B) A legal advisor.　　　　Did you hear the thunder?
　　　(C) An architect.
　　　(D) A banker.　　　　　　* listen 仔細聽

I listened carefully but I couldn't hear the

GO ON TO THE NEXT PAGE

thunder.

78. (D) What does the speaker say is a problem?
   (A) Some construction has not been completed. 有些建設還沒有完成
   (B) A warehouse is difficult to find. 有間倉庫很難找
   (C) An <u>inspection</u> will be postponed. 有個檢查會被延遲
   *inspect v.
   *n.
   (D) A price is higher than desired. 有個價格比想要的價格高

79. (C) What does the speaker ask the listener to do?
   (A) Submit a <u>deposit</u>. 繳交訂金
   (B) Sign a <u>waiver</u>. 簽棄權聲明書
   (C) Return the call <u>promptly</u>. 快速的回覆一個電話
   (D) Review a document carefully. 仔細地檢查一個文件

   *deposit n. 訂金.押金.存款
   * waiver n. 放棄.棄權證書 n. 免責條款.棄權條款
   * promptly adv. 迅速地.敏捷地

<u>**Questions 80 through 82** refer to the following broadcast.</u>

交通報導
Good afternoon, here's your WGBH-EM 105.9 <u>traffic report</u>. For anyone heading
任何要去市中心的人，整市巴工中心區會有20到30分鐘的延遲
downtown, there are 20 to 30-minute delays entering the central business district, and
交通回堵在圓型交流道   *intersection 10字路口
traffic is backed up on the <u>circle interchange</u>. As you know, our city is hosting the
如大所知,這個城市這週末要主辦年度藍草音樂實   今天傍晚將於 Citgo Mobile Arena
annual bluegrass music festival this weekend. It will kick off this evening at Citgo
開始   雖然還有些剩票   預訂它快賣完
Mobile Arena, and although there are some tickets left, it's expected to sell out. So, if
如果你這週末需要通勤到市區   我們強烈建議你搭公車或火車
you have to <u>commute</u> into the city this weekend, we strongly encourage you to take the
bus or the train.

*kick off 開球.開始
* commute v. 通勤
commuter n. 通勤者
+belt 通勤圈

80. (C) What is the main topic of the broadcast?
   (A) A <u>celebrity</u> interview. 名人訪問
   (B) A weather report. 天氣報告
   (C) A traffic update. 交通狀況更新
   (D) An international news story. 國際新聞消息

*back up
①塞車
②支持: Will you back me up?
③備分
④證實: Figures backed this up.
數字證明了這一點
⑤倒車
⑥積壓: Orders are really backed up this month.
這個月訂單積壓很多。

81. (B) According to the speaker, what will begin today?
   (A) A sports tournament. 運動錦標賽
   (B) A music festival. 音樂會
   (C) A conference.
   (D) A seasonal market. 季節性市集

82. (D) What does the speaker suggest that listeners do?
   (A) Arrive early. 早點到
   (B) Bring warm clothes. 帶溫暖的衣服
   (C) Purchase tickets online. 線上買票
   (D) Take public transportation. 搭公眾交通工具

62

Let's wrap up our weekly personnel department meeting with a staffing update for the St. Louis office. As you know, we've been working hard to fill several managerial positions there by the end of the year. And our policy is, of course, to promote from within. However, so far, most of the applications from qualified candidates are from outside the company and, well, the deadline to submit was May 15. So, in light of the situation, I want the team to start interviewing those few in-house candidates next week. Please refer to the interview schedule, which I emailed to all of you at the outset of this meeting.

83. (B) Who most likely is the speaker?
    (A) A computer programmer.
    (B) A personnel manager.
    (C) An accountant.
    (D) A real estate agent.

84. (C) What does the speaker mean when she says, "The deadline to submit was May 15"?
    (A) They missed a good hiring opportunity.
    (B) They need to verify some details.
    (C) They must move forward with a task.
    (D) They forgot to notify a colleague.

85. (B) According to the speaker, what will happen next week?
    (A) A policy will be implemented.
    (B) Interviews will begin.
    (C) Bonuses will increase.
    (D) A system upgrade will be completed.

Do you regularly use teleconferencing to connect with colleagues working in other locations? Introducing Corona Flash, an easy teleconferencing service at a fraction of the cost! Our service is a simple way to set up and conduct conference calls in the U.S. Canada, and around the world. Teleconferencing should be easy, and a conferencing company should be honest. That's why we've never had any hidden fees, contracts, or monthly charges. Collaborate with groups from anywhere, to anywhere, anytime. Corona Flash — We're the next level of audio conference calling service. Visit our website to watch a step-by-step video of how easy it is to use.

GO ON TO THE NEXT PAGE.

86. (C) What is Corona Flash?
(A) A store security system. 一個商店的安全系統
(B) An Internet service provider. 網路服務提供商
(C) A teleconferencing application. 電信會議 app(應用程式)
(D) A new brand of smartphone. 智慧型手機的新品牌

87. (D) What does the speaker mean when he says, "Teleconferencing should be easy and a conferencing company should be honest"?
(A) Employees need more training. 員工需要更多訓練
(B) Networks should be faster. 網路應該要更快
(C) An invoice should be reviewed. 有張發票需要被檢查
(D) Other systems are not as efficient. 其他的系統沒那麼有效率(能勝任)

*invoice 發票
* receipt 收據
* treasury invoice
VAT invoice

88. (C) What does the speaker say listeners can do on a website?
(A) Register a product. 註冊商品
(B) Make a purchase. 購買
(C) View a demonstration. 看示範
(D) Sign up for updates. 登記更新.升級

*register　　統一發票
①註冊 ②注意到. I didn't register.
③顯示 ④流露出
⑤公開發表, 正式發表. I decided to register a complaint with the manager.

Questions 89 through 91 refer to the following excerpt from a meeting.

我想要在氣氛最好的時候結束我們的每月員工會議
I wanted to end our monthly staff meeting on a high note. Now, if you haven't read the
如果你尚未閱讀Cleveland月報的商業版　　我很強烈地建議你讀一下
business section in today's *Cleveland Daily News*, I highly recommend that you do.
你會看到我們在大Cleveland區得到最棒數行行銷公司獎
You'll see there that we received the award for the best digital marketing company in
但不要忘了, 每天都有新公司開幕
the Greater Cleveland area. But keep in mind, there are new firms opening every day.
為了維持成功　　我們的生意必須成長　　我們租了更大的
In order to remain successful, our business has to grow. And so, we've leased a larger
空間　　我們也會僱情更多的人
space and will be hiring more people soon. Details of our move and expansion should
be finalized by the end of the month. 搬家的細節會在這個月底有結論出來。
和拓展

89. (A) What did the *Cleveland Daily News* recently do?
宣佈得獎者 (A) It announced award winners.
和別的報紙 (B) It merged with another newspaper.
合併 (C) It reviewed a group of restaurants. 審查一群餐廳 (像導覽)
(D) It reduced its subscription fee. 減少它的訂閱費

*reduce v. ①減少, 降低
② 把..毀壞
This beautiful forest has been reduced to a wastland.

90. (B) What has the business done recently?
(A) Bought a new property. 買一個新房子(辦公室)
(B) Leased a larger facility. 租個更大的地方
(C) Hired more staff. 僱用更多的員工
(D) Upgraded some computers. 升級一些電腦

③ The building was reduced to rubble.
dust.
ashes.
變為石碟. 灰燼.

91. (B) What does the speaker imply when he says, "There are new firms opening every day"? 一間分公司特會被建造

　　(A) A branch location will be built. 部競對手會增加
　　(B) Competition for customers will increase.
　　(C) More people will move to the area. 更多人會搬到這個區
　　(D) Road conditions will worsen. 路面狀況會更糟

bad – worse – worst
worsen v. 變得更糟

Questions 92 through 94 *refer to the following announcement.*

Greetings and welcome Spring Hill Mall shoppers! I'd like to direct your attention to the main atrium of our shopping mall today. In just 10 minutes, we're inviting you to join us there for a professional cooking demonstration. We'll be showcasing a variety of home cookware from different stores here in the mall. After the show, there'll be culinary experts on hand for those who have questions about cooking and how to buy and maintain the proper cookware. And, one of the housewares companies participating, Uptown Pantry, has just set up a new store on the ground floor. You're invited to attend their grand opening today.

我想把你們的注意力引導到
主要中庭(大廳)
10分鐘內, 我們邀致了有你來參加
專業的烹飪示範
我們特會展示不同的
家庭廚具 來自商場的不同店家
展示過後
會有烹飪專家在場 回答問題, 關於烹飪, 如何買, 維持合適的廚具
還有一家家用的公司會參加, 他們剛在
底層樓開店
(通常是一樓)
又 餐具至食品儲藏室

92. (C) Where is the announcement taking place?
　　(A) At a catering company headquarters. 外燴公司總部
　　(B) At a sports stadium. 運動場
　　(C) At a shopping mall. 購物中心
　　(D) At a restaurant. 餐廳裡

* culinary
adj. 烹飪的
廚房的

* expert
n. = adept = professional

93. (A) What does the speaker say will happen immediately after today's event?
　　(A) Experts will provide consultations. 專家會提供諮詢
　　(B) Attendees will fill out a survey. 參加者會填好一個調查
　　(C) A famous chef will speak. 有名的廚師會說話(演講)
　　(D) A meal will be served. 會提供餐點

94. (C) What does the speaker say about Uptown Pantry?
　　(A) It has won an award. 得過獎
　　(B) It has undergone a renovation. 有過一個整修
　　(C) It is now officially open. 現在正式開幕
　　(D) It is giving away free tickets. 有免費贈票

~ee 被~之人 重音皆在ee上
devotee n. 獻身者
employee n 員工
examinee n. 受試者
nominee n. 被提名者
referee n. 裁判
trainee n. 新兵

除了 committee 委員會
的重音不一樣

GO ON TO THE NEXT PAGE.

Guys, just a quick roundup before we open the bakery today. If you take a look at this chart, you'll see this week's winning pastry. As promised, the bakery item that got the most votes will be discounted by 25% for a week. I'd like to thank Daniel again for his creative idea of holding this weekly contest. Our customers are crazy about this promotion, and it has really increased sales. I know a lot of you have great ideas, too. Remember, you guys are always welcome to share.

95. (D) Look at the graphic. Which item will be discounted this week?
   (A) Cupcake.
   (B) Doughnut.
   (C) Scone.
   (D) Muffin.

BAKERY ITEM	# of votes
Muffin	503
Éclair	411
Scone	392
Doughnut	225
Cupcake	144

96. (A) Why does the speaker thank Daniel?
   (A) He proposed a sales promotion.
   (B) He developed new bakery items.
   (C) He worked extra hours.
   (D) He submitted an order.

97. (A) What does the speaker remind the listeners to do?
   (A) Make some suggestions.
   (B) Sign up for a task.
   (C) Clean some equipment.
   (D) Count customer votes.

*They'll be arriving by and by.
By and large, your idea is a good one.
by the way
by the by = old-fashioned

*submit
under | send
She refused to submit to his control.
I was not prepared to submit to this painful course of treatment.

這是SWG公司的自動電話系統通知您，您的
Hello, this is the automated call service from Syracuse Water and Gas reminding you

水電瓦斯帳單將在4月12日，週一到期　由於您的付款已超過10天
that your utility bill was due Monday, April 12. Since your payment is ten days

延遲費用已經加到您的帳戶餘額上(該帳戶要繳的全額上)
overdue, a late fee has been added to your account balance. Please pay the bill plus

請您上網繳交帳單和延遲費用
your ten-day late fee on our website at: "http://www.syracuse.gov". We also offer an

我們也有提供自動付款的特色(功能)在網站上　如果你註冊這項服務
auto payment feature on our website. If you sign up for this service, you will be

你將被要求提供信用卡和銀行帳戶號　登記之後，你未來的帳單
required to provide a credit card or bank account number. After that, your future bills

將會在到期那天自動付款
will be paid automatically on the day they are due. If you have questions about this

option, please call us at 717-922-7080. Thank you.　如果您對於這個選項有疑問

請致電 717-922-7080

98. (C) Where does the speaker most likely work?
(A) At a financial institution. 在財經機構
(B) At a water park. 在水上公園
(C) At a utility company. 公用事業詞
(D) At a bank. 銀行

大帳單
(美)吃飯帳單：Check, please.

99. (B) Look at the graphic. How much is the listener's late fee?
(A) $5.99.
(B) $12.98.
(C) $21.97.
(D) $30.96.

遲繳費是多少?
(英)吃飯帳單：Bill, please.
Put this on my bill. 記我帳上

bill 片語
→ fit the bill 符合需求、達到標準
Once you find someone to fit the bill,
just go ahead and hire them.
→ foot the bill = pay the bill
付錢/對某事負責

Late Payment Policy	
Days Overdue 過期	Fee
5	$5.99
10	$12.98
15	$21.97
20	$30.96

100. (D) What must the listener provide to sign up for a service?
(A) A medical certificate. 醫療的證書
(B) An identification card. 身份証
(C) Some contact information. 聯絡資訊
(D) Some payment details. 付款細節

Who is going to foot the
bill for the loss?
說要為這次損失負責(買單)

GO ON TO THE NEXT PAGE

READING TEST

In the Reading test, you will read a variety of texts and answer several different types of reading comprehension questions. The entire Reading test will last 75 minutes. There are three parts, and directions are given for each part. You are encouraged to answer as many questions as possible within the time allowed.

You must mark your answers on the separate answer sheet. Do not write your answers in your test book.

PART 5

Directions: A word or phrase is missing in each of the sentences below. Four answer choices are given below each sentence. Select the best answer to complete the sentence. Then mark the letter (A), (B), (C), or (D) on your answer sheet.

101. Simpson and Sons Landscaping has been ------- recommended by several neighboring businesses.
(A) high
(B) highly
(C) highest
(D) higher

102. Mrs. Watanabe wants to know when ------- shipment will be ready for delivery.
(A) her
(B) hers
(C) she
(D) herself

103. Due to the power outage, the marketing meeting has been rescheduled ------- tomorrow.
(A) at
(B) for
(C) in
(D) by

104. Trakstar's newest data collection algorithm makes it much ------- for business owners to generate mailing lists.
(A) easy
(B) easily
(C) easier
(D) easiest

105. By ------- retail locations in Beijing, Manila, and Kuala Lumpur, Carrington Ltd. has continued its growth into overseas markets.
(A) opens
(B) open
(C) opening
(D) opened

106. The ceramic tiles may be weakened ------- the kiln's heat is set too low.
(A) so
(B) if
(C) but
(D) why

107. Seven Miles High is the second ------- distributed in-flight magazine in the global airline industry.
(A) wide
(B) widen
(C) more widely
(D) most widely

108. Crazy Steve's Bar and Grill will be closed next weekend to accommodate a private -------.
(A) expense
(B) function
(C) customer
(D) occasion

14

109. Dr. Morgan Piersall, the keynote speaker at this year's National Fishing and Wildlife Expo, ------- several revolutionary depth location devices.
(A) enrolled
(B) communicated
(C) invented
(D) exceeded

110. During today's meeting, Ms. Robinson made a point of ------- the sales team for their exceptional results last month.
(A) congratulating
(B) congratulatory
(C) congratulation
(D) congratulate

111. The consumer satisfaction survey results are ------- to differ among age groups.
(A) likely
(B) probable
(C) recent
(D) important

112. Beginning October 31, the accounting department will issue sales commissions ------- from biweekly paychecks.
(A) separating
(B) separation
(C) separates
(D) separately

113. The course taught by Reed McIntyre is geared toward ------- students interested in computers or tech-related careers.
(A) which
(B) whose
(C) either
(D) those

114. Online debit card transactions are ------- in the user's account immediately.
(A) reflects
(B) reflecting
(C) reflect
(D) reflected

115. The new Fraud Alert program allows bank customers to ------- their account for any suspicious activity.
(A) monitored
(B) monitor
(C) monitoring
(D) monitors

116. Consult our press kit for facts and information ------- our company's colorful history.
(A) pending
(B) regarding
(C) within
(D) throughout

117. Please review the travel itinerary carefully ------- it has been received from the communications department.
(A) ever since
(B) as soon as
(C) then
(D) while

118. ------- of the service writer include detailed cost estimates and ensuring customer satisfaction.
(A) Productions
(B) Responsibilities
(C) Promotions
(D) Offerings

119. Our firm is dedicated to protecting the ------- of our clients' affairs.
(A) confiding
(B) confides
(C) confidential
(D) confidentiality

120. ------- an increase in affordable arc welders, metal sculpture has become a more accessible and popular art medium.
(A) Rather than
(B) Such as
(C) Due to
(D) Instead of

GO ON TO THE NEXT PAGE.

15

121. Our investment in LED light bulbs played a key _role_ in reducing our operating expenses by cutting down on electricity usage.
(A) basis
(B) agency
(C) factor
(D) role

122. The scheduled construction of a new subway station in Richland Village has created a _sizable_ demand for skilled workers.
(A) sizable
(B) durable
(C) lengthy
(D) tidy

123. The spokesperson stated that the buy-out was successfully completed ------- third-party arbitration.
(A) thanks to
(B) even if
(C) as well as
(D) overall

124. The marketing team for Vedder Sporting Goods is ------- a branding campaign to target younger consumers.
(A) considers
(B) consider
(C) considered
(D) considering

125. Last year, Cooper-Staubach Industries ------- an internship program for engineering students studying industrial aviation.
(A) signaled
(B) established
(C) demonstrated
(D) specialized

126. ------- a brief slump in summer sales, the Smile Motor Company exceeded second quarter earnings expectations.
(A) In case
(B) Because
(C) In spite of
(D) Concerning

127. The plan to ------- the Sioux City processing facility will have a significant impact on Honeybee Farm's overall poultry productivity.
(A) expansion
(B) expanded
(C) expanse
(D) expand

128. ------- being the critic's least favorite film at the Venice Film Festival, _Addicted to Love_ nevertheless won the People's Choice Award for best visual effects.
(A) Furthermore
(B) Without
(C) Despite
(D) Until

129. We found the Aloha Point-of-Sale (POS) solution to be the only system ------- for our needs.
(A) extensive
(B) adequate
(C) attractive
(D) deliberate

130. Mr. Gomez correctly predicted that sales would decrease ------- as the company scaled back on social media advertising.
(A) productively
(B) incrementally
(C) arguably
(D) reportedly

16

Directions: Read the texts that follow. A word, phrase, or sentence is missing in parts of the each text. Four answer choices are given below each of the text. Select the best answer to complete the text. Then mark the letter (A), (B), (C), or (D) on your answer sheet.

Questions 131-134 refer to the following article.

acquire v. 取得, 獲得, → acquire corporation enterprise 收購公司/企業
company

J.P. Esquire International to Acquire Constellation Technology

SEATTLE — J.P. Esquire International (JPEI) announced Wednesday that ___131.___ would purchase Constellation Technology in a deal valued at $250 million. *會以250個一百萬的價格 買下CT公司(21億5千萬)*

發言人
A spokesperson for JPEI said the company expects to double its profits by the end of next year. It will accomplish this by making full use of Constellation's recently updated production facilities. ___132.___ *(這招要放, 新公司好的內容)*

財務專家相信收購CT的舉動會讓JPEI
Financial experts believe the Constellation acquisition will make JPEI the world's leading producer of circuits. *線路* "They will be well ahead of their ___133.___ *competitors*." said top analyst Vince Rizzo. *1位 分析師*
成為世界領導的線路製造商, 會領先他們的

J.P. Esquire plans to maintain Constellation's current workforce *人力* with each of Constellation's factories continuing normal operations for the next five years. *After that time* ___134.___ JPEI will evaluate whether additional staff are needed.

發訊說公司預計在今年底把利潤變兩倍
藉由完整的運用CT公司最近更新的製造生產設備。讓CT公司的工廠都繼續正常運作
與JPEI公司計畫要維持CT公司目前的人力
接下來的5年
之後再評估是否需要多的員工 如你所要求的

131. (A) it
   (B) he
   (C) those
   (D) someone

(D) 另間公司提供的職缺被拒絕了
(C) 另外一間公司明年會被購買
(A) 這筆交易會改善士氣 (B) 所有四間都開展大生產量

132. (A) The transaction should improve morale
   (B) All four are operating at maximum capacity
   (C) Another company will be acquired next year
   (D) Offers from other firms were rejected

133. (A) critics
   (B) suppliers
   (C) investors
   (D) competitors

134. (A) As you requested
   (B) As a matter of fact *事實上*
   (C) After all *畢竟*
   (D) After that time *在那之後*

GO ON TO THE NEXT PAGE

shack n. 零食

①desert /dɪ'zɝt/ v. 逃跑、拋棄 ≠ dessert n. 點心 (正餐之後的甜點、水果)

All his friends have deserted him.

n. /dɛzɝt/ /oesɪs/ /ɪn/ 小旅館、小飯店

Desert Oasis Inn: Reservations 綠洲沙漠小旅店

We recommend reservations because hotel accommodations at the Desert Oasis Inn are (very) ~~limited~~ 我們建議要預約. 因為飯店的住宿非常有限。
135. (房間數不多, 客人太多都有可能)

Reservations will be held with a one-night deposit or 50 percent of total room charges for stays of longer than one night.
入住超過一晚, 將會收取一晚金額作為押金或是所有房費的 5%。

Cancellations made more than seven days prior to your scheduled arrival date will be refunded **------- in full.** 預訂入住7天前取消入住可獲得全額退款
136.

If, for some reason, a reservation must be cancelled within one week of your scheduled arrival date, charges for the entire length **------- of your stay will be billed**
137.

to you. -------. 若基於某些原因,
138. 在您預訂到達的日期一周內取消了房者, 所有住宿費用將會寄給您
(少於7天內取消, 收全額的意思啦!)

limit n. 界線、限度 He knows his own limits. 他知道自己的限度 (自知能力有限)
　　　v. 限制　　　We must limit ourselves to one steak each.
limitation n. 限制

135. (A) limits
(B) (B) limited
(C) limitation
(D) limiting

136. (A) are refunding
(C) (B) had been refunding
(C) will be refunded
(D) were refunded
希望能有個愉快的入住經驗 ←

137. (A) area
(C) (B) height
(C) length
(D) sense

這項政策適用於提早離開的住戶 (你早走, 我先說
138. (A) This policy applies to early departure as well 一樣收全額)
(D) (B) In addition, we will soon open another store in Oasis 另外, 我們馬上會開另一間店在綠洲
(C) We hope that you have enjoyed your stay
(D) Hotel guests are welcome to cancel at any time 飯店客人歡迎隨時取消

*allot = How many students finished the test in the alloted time?
勾學生在指定時間內完成考試?

place
locate
Computer <u>Funds</u> <u>Allocated</u>   allocate 指派,分配
基金,資金,專款,存款
allotment n. 配額

New technology is coming ------- the students of Arlington
                                139.
Heights. On Friday, Mayor Leland Morris announced
  數位就是未來   提案   被同意(通過) 宣布
that his "The Future is Digital" proposal was approved
  藍寧委員會
by the <u>Board of Supervisors</u> -------. The program <u>allots</u> 分配,拼發出
                                140.   撐和這個提案相關的
給每個學校15萬買電腦
$150,000 to each school in the city for the purchase of
computers. Students will be allowed to <u>take home</u> 拿回家的
                                     occasionally
laptops and tablets ------- for special assignments and
筆記型電腦   平板   141.   有特別的功課還有作業呀
class projects, but they will normally ------- to the students
                                       142. be available
only during school hours.
  但這些電腦通常只有上課期間可以使用(放暑.寒假呀不行)

141. (A) occasional 偶然的,偶爾的

(B) exceptional adj. 優異的,非凡的 Her scores were quite exceptional.
①特別的,格外的 These works of art must be handled with exceptional
②特別的,格外的   care.

139. (A) to   這些藝術品要特別小心拿   141. (A) occasionally
A   (B) at   A   (B) exceptionally
     (C) from ③例外的: It's an exceptional situation.   (C) finally
     (D) on (D) supposedly adv. 據說地   (D) supposedly
        → This house is supposedly haunted. 據說這房子鬧鬼

140. (A) The desks will be purchased at a discount   142. (A) are available
D   rate 用折價買桌子。最後決定下個月出來   C   (B) not available
     (B) The final decision is expected next month   (C) be available
     (C) Nevertheless, the mayor remains content   (D) were availed
        with the decision 不過,市長仍對這個決定保持滿意
     (D) The vote took place on Wednesday, July 6   * content adj. 滿意的,滿足的
        投票6月6日週三舉行

GO ON TO THE NEXT PAGE

144

cD) sequential adj. 按次序的 +file

December 2

Ms. Tracy Jordan

'sequel   n. 續集, 續篇

ASAP Travel Partners

4300 W. Armitage Avenue   sequence n. 一連串

Chicago, IL 60631

→ A computer can store and repeat sequences of instructions.

Dear Ms. Jordan,   → Are the numbers in sequence? 按順序

謝謝你在聖人辦公室購買的10盒碳粉盒 ⊤

Thank you for your purchase of 10 Fratello GN460 High-Yield Black

碳粉盒 義大利人鑄賽

Toner Cartridges from Office Oracle. Your online order was received

on December 1 and is ready for shipping. --D.

你的線上訂單以收到,已準備好派送   143. → 要接和訂單有關的

We appreciate that you have chosen Office Oracle for your

辦事的 company's clerical and office needs. As a show of thanks, we are

書記的 applying a 10 percent discount to this ---particular--- order. ---Additionally---, we are

這比特定的訂單打9折   144.   145.

including a reimbursement of shipping charges. Enclosed you will

find the adjusted invoice and a check for $17.50.

除此之外,我們還補償運費,這函附件你會看到調整過的發票和17.5的支票

Office Oracle is pleased to welcome you to the family and ------(D)

期待未來提供給你有品質的產品和服務   146. ↗ looks forward

providing you with quality products and service in the future.

Sincerely,   * reimbursement   * yield

Udee Aritisi   n. 退款, 賠償, 補償   屈服 → He didn't yield himself to

Customer Service Representative   his rival. 他並未屈服於對手

Enclosure   *toner 碳粉, 調色劑, 化妝粉

感謝你有興趣來上班

143. (A) Your interest in employment opportunities
with us is appreciated 很不幸地, 我們寫信提醒

(B) Unfortunately, we are writing to inform you
of a delay in delivery 你有吭運送會延達

(C) However, it seems that you have failed to
reply 然而, 看起來你回覆失敗了

(D) You may expect to receive your order in
5-7 business days 5-7天工作日你可能會收到包裹

144. (A) ongoing 進行中的 + discussion 討論
(B) complimentary   Investment 投資   (B) 免費的
(C) particular   study 研究   (C) 特殊的, 特定的 ↗ 我沒異議, 我不管
(D) sequential (up)   <D> I'm not particular spoken.

145. (A) For example
(B) Still
(C) However
(D) Additionally

146. (A) leaves room
(B) pushes harder
(C) goes back
(D) looks forward

Directions: In this part you will read a selection of texts, such as magazine and newspaper articles, e-mails, and instant messages. Each text or set of texts is followed by several questions. Select the best answer for each question and mark the letter (A), (B), (C), or (D) on your answer sheet.

* handy adj. 手邊的 ② 好用的: a handy tip/hint
③ 便利的: A vacuum cleaner is a handy household tool.

Questions 147-148 refer to the following invoice.

位於區 #downtown 市中心 (商業區)

④ 靈巧的: He is handy with words.

UPTOWN THEATER
1001 Broadway Avenue
Easton

Invoice #: 0411-5662-UT *善於辭令

發票號要放在手邊(保存好,會用到)
*Keep this invoice number <u>handy</u>. You will need it if you have to contact customer service. 如果要聯絡客服.就用得到.

收到要去Uptown Theater 的弟,199.88元,信用卡後4碼5622
Received from Carl Culver: $199.98 payment to Uptown Theater, charged to credit card ending in xxxx-5622

Description: Tickets for Bill Derby Trio in concert Saturday, April 11. Doors at 7:30 P.M.

連奏   現場
注意事項: 發票列印出來帶在身上,帶去現場.   集合地
IMPORTANT: Please print this invoice and bring it with you to the venue. No paper invoice will be mailed. Be sure to arrive early to check your name on the preorder list at the ticket counter. Visit our website for our ticket refund policy.

不要寄紙本發票給你

請確認早點到場 確認預購的名字. 退票政策
* identification   到票亭   請上網看。

n.① 身份證   憑指紋確認罪犯
② 認出,識別: the identification of criminals by their fingerprints

147. What does Mr. Culver plan to do on April 11?
(A) Call the theater. 打給電影院
(B) Travel abroad. 出國旅行
(C) Pay his credit card bill. 付信用卡帳單
(D) Attend a musical event. 參加音樂節

148. What must Mr. Culver bring with him?
(A) A credit card.
(B) Paper tickets. 紙本票券
(C) A copy of an invoice. 複印的發票
(D) A form of identification. 身份證明表格

GO ON TO THE NEXT PAGE.

●●●●○ AT&T 🛜   9:18 PM   🔒 ✈ ⏱ 76% 🔋

❮ Messages   **Rick Lancer**   Details

安裝新的聲音系統

Maria, I'm at the Armitage Hotel, installing the
new sound system. Raphael called in sick, and
一打來請病假

這個工作太複雜無法自己完成
this job is too complicated to do alone. It's not

這不是我所預想的狀況   這是一個大空間被
what I expected. It's a large space that can be

分成幾個小的房間   飯店想要
divided into smaller rooms, and the hotel wants

一個可以程式化的系統，當場地同時被安排一個會議或晚宴
a programmable system to work when the space

使用時就可以運作。
is used for more than one meeting or dinner

scheduled at the same time. Can you get in

touch with Gary Winters and ask him to come

help me? I don't have his mobile phone number.

* divide v. 分. 割. 除   * make a call   打電話
12 divided by 4 equals 3   take/answer a call 接電話
                         return a call   回電
* call in sick 打電話請病假

pull a sickie 裝病   an incoming call   來電
                           outgoing call   撥出去的電話
→ He pulled a sickie to go to the
football game.   * pay a call on sb. 拜訪某人
                           pay sb. a call
他裝病去看足球比賽

149. What problem does Mr. Lancer have?   **150.** Why did Mr. Lancer send the text
A   (A) He is unable to do a job by   C   message to Maria?
      himself. 他無法自己完成一份工作
                                (A) To have her reschedule a meeting
     (B) He feels sick and cannot work. 覺得不舒服   at a hotel. 重新安排在飯店的會議
                        不能工作
     (C) He will not be able to attend a   (B) To cancel an event in the hotel
      scheduled meeting. 不能參加一個   ballroom. 取消飯店舞的活動
     (D) He does not know how to contact 安排好的 (C) To ask her to make a call. 要她打電話
      a vendor. 他不知如何聯絡   會議
                                 (D) To request special equipment.
        一個賣家   要求特別來的設備

*swank v. 吹牛、炫耀 to swank about sth.
adj. 華麗的、愛打扮的

The Swank Oasis Hotel & Spa
又 Oe 綠洲 →客戶滿意度調查

CUSTOMER SATISFACTION SURVEY

感謝光入住,客戶滿度對我們來說很重要.感謝您的回饋(填意見表)
Thank you for staying at the Swank Oasis Hotel & Spa. Customer satisfaction is very important to us, and we would appreciate your feedback. Please fill out the survey below and leave it with the receptionist at the front desk when you check out.

請把下列3個表表填完.交給框台接待人員當你退房呼
How satisfied were you with the Swank Oasis Hotel & Spa?

Please circle one selection for each category:

SERVICE 服務	Not satisfied	Satisfied	(Very Satisfied)
CLEANLINESS 清潔	Not satisfied	Satisfied	(Very Satisfied)
APPEARANCE 外觀	Not satisfied	Satisfied	(Very Satisfied)
RESTAURANT 餐廳	Not satisfied	(Satisfied)	Very Satisfied

會推應飯店給朋友嗎?
Would you recommend the Swank Oasis Hotel & Spa to others?

No   Maybe   (Yes)

Please add any comments or suggestions you may have in the space below:

整體而言 我有個高度滿意的經驗
All in all, I had a highly satisfactory experience at the Hotel & Spa. The hotel 飯店員工非常和善 Spa非常乾淨 舒適
employees were extremely friendly. The spa was very clean and comfortable.
謝謝完次的設備 可以享受放鬆的一天
Thanks to the well-equipped facilities, I was able to enjoy a relaxing stay. The restaurant, however, though inexpensive, was not particularly memorable. adj.難忘的
餐廳 雖然不貴但 沒有特別印象

If you wish to be contacted with promotional offers, please provide your name and phone number or e-mail address.

(A)他是有經驗的 masseuse. 女按摩師
/mæˈsɜs/

Steve Bruges   s_bruges@ivria.com

(B)他想在飯店業工作

1)告訴朋友們這間飯店

151. What are guests asked to do?
C (A) Tell their friends about the hotel.
   (B) Recommend staff members for awards. 推應員工得獎品
   (C) Return a completed form. 交回填完的表搭
   (D) Leave their keys at the front desk. 前台(框台)

152. What is suggested about Mr. Bruges?
C (A) He is an experienced masseuse.
   (B) He would like a job in the hotel industry. 他會再次入住了
   (C) He would stay at the hotel again.
   (D) He would like to discuss his stay with hotel staff.
   他會和員工討論他的住宿

GO ON TO THE NEXT PAGE.

Questions 153-154 refer to the following online chat discussion.

Linda Chevalier 4:04 P.M. 我從來沒有參加過線上訓練課. 我就去休傳給我的網址
I've never participated in a training session online. I just go to the website address you e-mailed me, and click the Join button, right? 然後按 "加入" 鈕就好了, 對吧?

Gus LaMotta 4:02 P.M. 沒錯. 然後你需要輸入進入密碼
Correct. Then you'll need to enter the access code:AXCORP. *deny v.否定, 拒絕

Linda Chevalier 4:04 P.M. 一個跳出視窗告訴我這個訊息 "錯誤碼. 拒絕進入"
A pop-up window gave me this message. "Error Code: 404. Access Denied." Is that the right code? 那是對的代碼嗎? *pop-up 自出, 突然跳起

Gus LaMotta 4:05 P.M. 讓我再次確認. 可能有錯
Let me double-check. Might be a mistake. *issue
n. 問題. 期刊. 發行物
3女 → He died without issue.

Linda Chevalier 4:05 P.M. 或是有可能網站有問題?
Or maybe there's an issue with the website? v.發行, 發次, 配給

Gus LaMotta 4:06 P.M. 是我的錯. 我給了你會議代碼而不是進入代碼
Yeah. My bad. I gave you the meeting code instead of the access code. Try EVANSTON.

確認你的音響裝置是打開的.
按 "使用視訊" 鈕在螢幕上面右邊
Linda Chevalier 4:07 P.M. 你會看見聽到訓練師. 他也會.
Bingo! Thanks. 可以了, 謝 要去除背景雜音, 你可能想要把麥克風開靜音
直到要說話的時候.

Gus LaMotta 4:08 P.M.
Great. Make sure your audio is on. Click the ENABLE WEB CAM button at the top right of the screen. You'll see and hear the trainer, and vice versa. To eliminate v.排除.消
background noise, you may want to mute your microphone until prompted to speak. 除
開靜音   v.促使.激起

(A) 訓練已經完成

153. At 4:06 P.M., what does Mr.
C   LaMotta most likely mean when he writes, "My bad"?
   (A) The training has been accomplished. 網站不能用
   (B) The Web site is unavailable.
   (C) He made a mistake. 犯了個錯
   (D) He thought of something else.

他想成其他事

154. What is probably true about Mr. LaMotta?
D   (A) He has recently received a new computer. 最近收到新電腦
   (B) He does not have permission to attend the meeting. 沒有參加會議的許可
   (C) He often participates in conference calls. 常參加電話會議
   (D) He is familiar with the training session. 對訓練課很熟

24

Duggar Elite Systems, LLC

1301 Punchbowl St, Honolulu, HI 96813, USA

Invoice: DES-982354	Shipped on: June 19

Billed to:	Dr. Virgil Spires
	Straub Medical Center
	Hawaii Pacific University Hospital
	888 S King St, Honolulu, HI 96810, USA

Item Code	Description	Quantity
6SNUGS4	Polyurethane Dressing	15
3HSINM3***	Tracheotomy Barrier Shield	25
2NONDM7	Drain Sponge (50 ct.)	10
9DDOCK0	Surgical Gloves (100 ct.)	60

***Item 3HSINM3 will be delivered at a later date because they are currently not in the warehouse.

---

155. What most likely is Duggar Elite Systems?
- (A) A clothing manufacturer.
- (B) A medical supply company.
- (C) A hospital.
- (D) A doctor's office.

156. According to the invoice, what happened on June 19?
- (A) A payment was refunded.
- (B) A shipment was delivered.
- (C) An invoice was revised.
- (D) An order was shipped.

157. What is indicated about the barrier shields?
- (A) They are out of stock at the moment.
- (B) They are available in one color only.
- (C) They are no longer manufactured.
- (D) They are the wrong size.

GO ON TO THE NEXT PAGE.

Questions 158-160 refer to the following memo.

To: All Staff
From: Jeffrey Perlman
Re: Office Expenses
Date: Monday, October 3

We've all seen the expense report from last quarter, and it is clear that we need to reduce our costs on office supplies.

So, it's pretty obvious that we can start saving immediately on printing and copying documents.

Not to point any fingers, but a number of us have been making color copies of general documents, such as travel itineraries, prototype drafts, and deadline schedules. ---[1]--- Purchasing frequent replacements inevitably leaves us with less money to spend on things like business travel and social events. ---[2]---

While we could implement a system wherein all jobs must first be approved by the department supervisors, I would prefer that employees make their own decisions about printing and copying. ---[3]---

Please reserve the use of color for only those cases where visual appeal is a significant factor. Publicity flyers intended for clients are one obvious example. ---[4]---

Thank you for your attention to this matter.

158. What is one purpose of the memo?
(A) To inform a staff of an error in a document.
(B) To request cooperation with a departmental procedure.
(C) To delay the release of a quarterly expense report.
(D) To alert employees to a budget concern.

159. What are employees advised to do?
(A) Distribute travel itineraries by e-mail.
(B) Get prior approval from their supervisors.
(C) Make black and white copies of basic documents.
(D) Tell co-workers about upcoming social events.

160. In which of the positions marked [1], [2], [3], and [4] does the following sentence best belong?

"While multicolor documents are more attractive and eye-pleasing than black-and-white, color ink cartridges are pricy and inefficient."

(A) [1].
(B) [2].
(C) [3].
(D) [4].

26

Recycling Survey in Progress

Many St. Claire residents, businesses and visitors have expressed concerns to town officials about inadequate recycling facilities. ---[1]--- With a data-collection project scheduled to begin on Tuesday, led by Moogley Associates of St. Claire, town officials will soon learn the extent of the recycling output on a typical weekday, during the evening, and at peak times when events are taking place in town. ---[2]--- When it is completed, the study will provide updated statistics of all public and private recyclable material produced in the area and typical rates of disposal. ---[3]--- "The general consensus is that the demand has increased with the four businesses and the two residential developments we've seen in the last five years," said Planning Director Maria Stotts. "But we need hard data before we can consider another costly recycling facility." ---[4]---

161. How many recycling centers are currently in St. Claire?
(A) one
(B) two
(C) four
(D) five

162. In which of the positions marked [1], [2], [3], and [4] does the following sentence best belong?
"Some have called for construction of a second recycling center in the next two years."
(A) [1].
(B) [2].
(C) [3].
(D) [4].

163. What does the article indicate about the survey?
(A) It will study the demand for recycling in three local neighborhoods.
(B) It will measure the demand for recycling at various times.
(C) It will be paid for by Moogley Associates of St. Claire.
(D) It will be conducted by St. Claire's planning director.

GO ON TO THE NEXT PAGE.

Questions 164-167 refer to the following article.

Start-Up Guru Coming to Laramie

LARAMIE (March 9) - Evan Smith, dubbed the "Bill Gates of startups" by the *Wyoming Tribune Eagle*, will be the keynote speaker at the 12th annual Laramie Small Business Expo (LSBE). The Expo will take place at the Wyoming Civic Center from April 13 to April 16. More than 1,000 start-up entrepreneurs will attend workshops and showcase their businesses at booths, where visitors can examine products and ask questions. According to an LSBE press release, Mr. Smith will feature many of the ideas from his bestselling book "The Art of the Startup" published just last year. Mr. Smith believes that there are several key decisions that must be made before launching any new business scheme. "You can't be starting from the idea of creating a product you want to sell," Mr. Smith writes in his book.

"The golden rule is to create a product people want to buy. And it is unquestionably crucial to get this right if you want your business to succeed."

Mr. Smith is the owner of several successful businesses in Portland, where he has lived for the past decade. "I was born and raised in Laramie," Mr. Smith said. "So I wanted to give back to the community where I got my start in any way I could, which is why I accepted the invitation to participate in the Expo. There's an outstanding opportunity there for start-up entrepreneurs. Following the simple but ultimately effective guidelines in my book worked well for me and for many other successful start-ups." Admission to the Expo is $20 per day, but tickets can be purchased for $15 in advance through LSBE's website at: www.lsbe.com/expo.

164. What is the article mainly about?
(A) A business figure's participation in an event.
(B) The drawbacks of running a small business.
(C) The opening of a start-up.
(D) New trends in marketing.

165. Why did Mr. Smith decide to participate in the Expo?
(A) He wants to support entrepreneurs in his hometown.
(B) He is doing research for a new training seminar.
(C) He would like to recruit some investors.
(D) He is looking for ways to increase production.

166. What does Mr. Smith say is the most important consideration for new entrepreneurs?
(A) Manufacturing a product in a cost-effective way.
(B) Creating a product that the business owner feels passionate about.
(C) Marketing a product on social media.
(D) Developing a product that is desired by consumers.

167. According to the article, what has Mr. Smith recently done?
(A) He survived a major accident.
(B) He traveled to Laramie.
(C) He wrote a book.
(D) He presented an award.

Ⅲ Grayson

grayson.com

Ⅲ Grayson

Your Opinion Is Important to Us

The Grayson Corporation has been conducting public opinion polls on current affairs since 1974.

All our polls are based on telephone interviews with adults 18 years of age or older who live in specific polling regions. To ensure that every adult living within a polling area has an equal chance of being contacted, potential interviewees are selected by a computer algorithm that generates phone numbers from all telecom networks.

To find out what people think about what is happening in the world these days, visit our Hot List page. New polls are published weekly, and all polls are stored and accessible online. If you prefer to search for polls by subject, go to our A-Z Directory page. If you would like to reproduce tables, charts, or any other graphics created by Grayson, go to the **Contact Us** page and click the link for our Licensing Division. There you will find an easy-to-use online form to fill out with details about how and where you intend to use the information. In most cases, a response is provided within 24 hours of submission.

168. In paragraph 1, line 2 the word "affairs" is closest in meaning to
(A) proposals.
(B) contracts.
(C) relationships.
(D) issues.

169. What is NOT mentioned about poll participants?
(A) They are interviewed over the phone.
(B) They are adults.
(C) They are randomly selected.
(D) They are interviewed in groups.

170. What is indicated about the Grayson Corporation?
(A) It is searching for new markets.
(B) It publishes telephone directories.
(C) It updates its website every week.
(D) It has offices in multiple locations.

171. How can readers get permission to reproduce graphics?
(A) By submitting a paper form.
(B) By providing information online.
(C) By visiting a retail location.
(D) By making a phone call.

GO ON TO THE NEXT PAGE

我剛進到會議室，投影機使用時遇到些問題，一直關機，有人知道為什麼嗎？

Vincent Ellerbosch [5:52 P.M.] *projector*
n. 投影機   projection → population projection 人口預測
n. 投影，設計   profit projection 利潤預測

Hi, everyone. I just got in the conference room, and I am having some trouble with the <u>projector</u>. It keeps shutting off. Does anyone know why?

我上次也遇到這個問題，試著按按灰色重置鍵
Onat Cheetslong [5:55 P.M.]
This happened to me last time. Try pushing the gray reset button.

所有事情不是應該今天下午3:30前安置好嗎？
Natalie Goff [5:55 P.M.]
Wasn't everything <u>supposed to</u> be set up by 3:30 this afternoon? I hope we'll be able to get everything ready before the board members

我希望我們可以在董事會員開始到達前把所有事用好   start arriving.

Vincent Ellerbosch [5:58 P.M.]   Glynn 應該要處理好，但是那種有另外一個會議而且開起超過時間了，她等不及了，所以她請我一但房間
Glynn Davis <u>was supposed to</u> do it, but there was another meeting in the room and it ran late. She couldn't wait, so she asked me to set up once the room was free.   清空就開始安置。

* come down
① 倒塌 ② 雨器下
③ 價格，溫度下降

Vincent Ellerbosch [5:59 P.M.]   你可以下樓來一趟嗎？
No, it doesn't work. Onat, can you <u>come down</u> here?

④ 流傳：The story was came down from time immemorial.

* be supposed to
現在式 = 應該 = should = ought to
過去式 = 本該發生卻沒發生 = should have Upp.
                                     ought to have Upp.

Onat Cheetslong [5:50 P.M.] 流傳
在路上了   On my way.   下來。 久遠以前

Natalie Goff [5:51 P.M.]
Are you all set otherwise?
那其他東西你都安置好了嗎？

報告要用的東西都好了。我請幾個同事試跑過了
Vincent Ellerbosch [5:52 P.M.] 確認每件事都清楚，我也把把報告要用的，董事會成員要的
Yes, Natalie, everything is ready for the presentations. I ran them by a few 資料
colleagues to make sure that everything is clear. I've made <u>hard copies</u> of 都印好了。
the presentation and the report which the board members will receive.

*hard copy 即印出來的紙本
不是用郵件或者其他方式

30

[handwritten: sharp]

[handwritten: 我8點整會到,帶大家去吃飯.然後把他們帶到各自的飯店]

Natalie Goff [5:55 P.M.]

Good. I will be there at 8:00 P.M. sharp to take everyone to dinner and then to their <u>respective</u> hotels. I will distribute the reports then too, so please make sure that they are completed before then. I will bring the group back tomorrow morning at 9:30 for the demo and closing sessions.

[handwritten: 我到時也會把報告發下去,所以請確定到時印好83]

[handwritten: 我會在隔天早上9:30把大家帶回來,看展示和閉幕]

Vincent Ellerbosch [5:59 P.M.]

[handwritten: 投影機現在好3. Onat 接3不同的電源線]

Thanks. The projector is working fine now. Onat attached a different <u>power cord</u>. *[handwritten: 電源線]*

[handwritten: 174(A)招呼一些董事會頭]

*[handwritten: * P.34 和 election 相關補充   diret eleetion]*
[handwritten: 台灣: 公民 citizen 常ID去vote → 直接選舉]
[handwritten: (B) 在飯店和 Goff 小姐見面]
[handwritten: 美國: general election]
[handwritten: (C) 結束檢查一些幻燈片]
[handwritten: (D) 去幫 Ellerbosch 先生]
[handwritten: 由民眾選出各州的選舉候選人 elector candidate, 再由選上的 elector 投票給總統候選人]
[handwritten: 稱選舉人團制度 electoral college]
[handwritten: 勝者全拿制 the winner take all   ↔ absolute majority system]
[handwritten: 相對多數當選 simple plurality system / relative plurality system]

172. What is Mr. Ellerbosch trying to do?
[handwritten: D]
(A) Train new employees. *[handwritten: 訓練新員工]*
(B) Meet with Ms. Goff.
(C) Copy some documents. *[handwritten: 複製些文件]*
(D) Prepare a room for a meeting. *[handwritten: 為了開會準備房間]*

173. Why was the conference room not set up by 3:30 P.M.?
[handwritten: D]
(A) Because Ms. Davis was not at work. *[handwritten: 不在上班,不在辦公室]*
(B) Because the new employees arrived late. *[handwritten: 新員工遲到]*
(C) Because the projector had not been located. *[handwritten: 投影機沒被找到]*
(D) Because a meeting did not end on time. *[handwritten: 會議沒有準時結束]*

174. At 5:50 P.M., what does Mr. Cheetslong most likely mean when he writes, "On my way"?
[handwritten: D]
(A) He is greeting some board members.
(B) He will meet Ms. Goff at the hotel.
(C) He will finish reviewing some slides.
(D) He is coming to help Mr. Ellerbosch.

175. What will happen at 8:00 P.M.?
[handwritten: C]
(A) Board members will listen to a presentation. *[handwritten: 聽報告]*
(B) Board members will return from the security office. *[handwritten: 從警衛室回來]*
(C) Ms. Goff will go to the conference room. *[handwritten: 去會議室]*
(D) Mr. Ellerbosch will complete some forms. *[handwritten: 把些表格填完成]*

GO ON TO THE NEXT PAGE

Wendy Jurassic
928 East Avon Avenue
Woodland Hills, MI 58902

May 20

Dear Ms. Jurassic,

We sincerely appreciate you coming in to interview for the senior Web administrator position at Forkel & Associates. However, I regret to inform you that the personnel department decided to go with another candidate. Nevertheless, we were impressed by the knowledge and experience that you displayed during your interview and have decided to offer you another recently-vacated position.

In contrast to the position you applied for, this position is part-time. You would be working on Tuesday, Wednesday, and Friday from 1 to 5 PM and on Monday and Thursday from 2 to 6 PM. Your responsibilities would include maintaining domain security, updating server patches, analyzing Web logs, and developing a content management system.

If you are interested in this position, please call me at 555-0923 or e-mail me at k_neierbaum@forkel.com.

Sincerely,
Kurtz Neierbaum

Handwritten annotations:

* log n. (航空/海) 日誌
web + log → weblog → blog
* logue 字根：說
monologue n. 獨白, 長篇大論
catalogue n. 目錄
colloquial adj. 口語的 說話的
obloquy n. 責罵
dialogue n. 對話
誠摯的感謝你來面試
遺憾的通知你 選擇 人事部門 決定 另外一位候選人 不過,
我們對於你在面試時表現出的知識和經驗印象深刻. 所以決定給你另一個最近空出來的職缺。和你之前申請的職位相照,這次是兼職
maintain v. 維持
domain n. 區域
工作內容包含:維護區域安全,更新伺服器補丁,分析部落格和研發令人滿意的管理系統
* patch n. 補丁.
電腦使用上：a small computer program that can be added to an existing program in order to make the existing program work as it should.

32

From:	Wendy Jurassic <r_jurassic@inmail.com>
To:	Kurtz Neierbaum <k_neierbaum@forkel.com>
Re:	Part-time opportunity 兼差機會
Date:	May 23

Dear Mr. Neierbaum

關於你5月20號的信. 很不幸地我申請的職位被填滿(已有人應徵上)

I'm writing with regard to your letter of May 20. It's unfortunate that the

我非常開心可以接受新職位你所提供的
position I applied for has been filled, but I would be very pleased to

但是   我在想   wonder v.
accept the new position that you are offering. However, I was wondering 納悶

想知道
if you would be agreeable to a minor change regarding the hours I would

宜的. 欣然贊同的   您是否能接受關於我工作時間的
be working.

我面試的時候, 我有提及在世界展望的 一些小小改變。→ 志工經歷
During my interview, I referenced my experience volunteering with

他們最近�給我
World Vision. I was recently offered a position working part-time for

一個兼差工作
them, but there is a schedule conflict. I work for them Tuesday,

Wednesday, and Thursday from 9 AM to 1 PM. Would it be possible for

me to work for you from 1:30 to 5:30 PM on Tuesday and Wednesday?

請你們一有空便通知我
If so, please let me know at your earliest convenience.

順帶提一句,   我在世界展望的工作內容和你們公司要我做的 完全一樣,
Incidentally, the duties that I currently perform for World Vision are

exactly the same as the responsibilities of the position with Forkel &

Associates. So, I believe that I would adjust very quickly to working for

所以我相信, 我會非常快的進入狀況
Forkel.

adjust v. 調整 改變~以適應

I look forward (to) becoming a valuable member of Forkel & Associates.

介系詞 to   ＊補充
Sincerely,

廠商: factory, supplier, vendor
Wendy Jurassic

物品明細 item description

總額: total amount

176. For what type of position did Ms. Jurassic apply for? 他申請的是何種職位？
D
(A) Legal assistance. 法務援助
(B) Graphic design. 圖像設計
(C) Accounting. 會計
(D) Information technology. 資訊科技

177. In the letter, the phrase "In contrast to" in paragraph 2, line 1 is closest on meaning to
D
(A) supporting. 支持 support
(B) against. 反對
(C) identical. adj. 完全相同的 → They look identical.
(D) unlike. adj. 不同的
他們長得一樣

178. What is suggested about Forkel & Associates?
D
(A) It has opened a new retail location. 要開新零售點
(B) It opens at 1 P.M. on certain days of the week. 這週有指定幾天下午1:00開
(C) It has signed several new clients. 記下幾位新客戶
(D) It recently hired a full-time employee. 最近僱用了全職員工

179. Why was the e-mail written? 第二篇
C
(A) To recommend someone for a position. 推薦某人一個職位
(B) To clarify information about a volunteer opportunity.
(C) To request an adjustment to a job schedule.
(D) To negotiate the salary being offered for a job.

180. What most likely is NOT a task Ms. Jurassic does at World Vision?
C
(A) Update the server. 更新伺服器
(B) Manage content. 管理內容
(C) File tax forms. 申報稅表
(D) Analyze Web logs. 分析部落格

* identity
v. 認同
identical
有關~的，~性的
(有認同性的) → adj. 相同的
identification
n. 認出、確認、身分證

* 總統選舉相關 (搭配 P.31)
台: 美都是總統制. Presidential System
但是推派方式不一樣
(台) 先被提名 nominate
→ 各黨內部初選 primary election
→ 或是公民聯署 countersign
(美): 內部初選.
→ 全國黨大會上確認 National party convention

179.
(B) 解釋志願職位的一些資訊
clarity v. 澄清、淨化、闡明

(C) 對於工作行程要求一個調整

(D) 討論新職務的薪水
negotiate v. 談判、協商

民主黨: The Democratic Party
共和黨: The Republican Party

34

員工年度表現審查報告
Employee Report for Annual Performance Review

DuPont 自然歷史博物館
DuPont Museum of Natural History

Conservation and Collections Department 保留 & 收集部

不有 { 同些
n. 保存、保護、管理 （自然資源永恆使用）
^area
preservation
n. 保護、保留、維持

*major
adj: 較大的、較多的
重要的、一流的

Name: Dana Mayberry

Title: Associate Scientist II

請列下今年你有參與的所有大案子 （現在有的資源保留）
Please list all major projects in which you participated this year:

1. Conducted two-week course in archaeological site preservation for
   university students majoring in Paleontology. (Feb 5-Feb 19)
   考古學的 /ˌɑːrkɪəˈlɑːdʒɪkl/ /ˌpeɪliɑːnˈtɑːlədʒɪ/
   執行 2 週的課程在考古學的保護區，為 30 念古生物學的大學主辦的。 古生物學

2. Represented Department of Conservation and Collections at
   Archaeological Institute of America (AIA) annual Conference on
   Natural History, Albany, NY. (March 20-March 24)
   自然
   於歷史博物館，AIA 舉辦的年度會議上介紹 C&C 部門

3. Presented paper, "Building a Strong Future for Archaeological
   拓展
   延伸
   Outreach and Education", at the AIA 2-day working conference in
   New Orleans, LA. (May 22-23)
   在 AIA 2 天於紐奧良的會中呈現報告(研究) → 建立考古學的延伸和教育的強大未來。

4. Conducted research on illicit antiquities found in major national
   collections. (April-Sept) Article was submitted to Journal of World
   禁止的
   illicit adj. 違法的
   Archaeology and accepted for publication.
   對於在這國家收藏中發現的違業古器物做研究，文章被收錄出版 antiquity n. 古代
   古器物

5. Led tours on weekends during opening celebration of new Dinosaur
   exhibition. (Nov 1-Nov 30)
   新的恐龍展 開幕慶典帶領隊伍參觀，週末時

GO ON TO THE NEXT PAGE.

Dana Mayberry of Evanston Receives Award

Evanston 的 Dana 接收獎

— Yale T. Briggs, Local News Reporter

這是贊揚 Dana 的貢獻和努力.
很開心有他在我們的團隊裡

[CHICAGO] January 23 — Evanston native Dana Mayberry has received the Hope Lawler Award from the Archaeological Institute of America *AIA* for her research on archaeological education. She works at the DuPont Museum of Natural History as an associate scientist. *副科學家*

Davidson Perry-Watts, director of the DuPont Museum, said that it is very rare for the award to be given to a scientist so early in her career. It is a *很少人可以在此行沒多久就得到這個獎* tribute to Dana's dedication and hard work, said Mr. Perry-Watts. "We are very happy to have her on our team."

Ms. Mayberry began work as a researcher after receiving a Master's degree in museum studies at Iowa /aɪəwə/ State University. She is a graduate of Lake Forest High School. *a graduate in law* *法律系畢業生*

The award will be presented on March 18 at the annual AIA Conference on Natural History, this year held in Las Vegas, NV.

181(A) 參加研究的新課程 (B) 開始新工作
(C) 基於他的研究做演講 (D) 做銷售發表

181. According to the report, why did Ms. Mayberry go to New Orleans?
C
(A) To enter a new course of study.
(B) To begin a new job.
(C) To give a talk based on her research.
(D) To make a sales presentation.

報告說博物館 11月會發生什麼事?

182. What does the report suggest happened at DuPont Museum in November?
C
(A) A conference was held. *會議*
(B) A multimedia system was finally replaced. *多媒體系統終於被取代(更新)*
(C) A new exhibition was opened. *新展開始*
(D) A research project was conducted. *(恐龍)*
研究案開始進行

這章最有可能在哪裡出現?

183. Where did the article most likely appear?
D
(A) In a promotional booklet. *宣傳手冊*
(B) In a museum brochure. *博物館手冊*
(C) In a scientific journal. *科學期刊*
(D) In a town newspaper. *小鎮報紙*

184(A) 納稅人資助的 (B) 通常: 頒給資深人員
(C) 是最高榮譽 (D) 每10年只頒一次

184. What does the article imply about the Hope Lawler Award?
B
(A) It is funded by taxpayers.
(B) It is usually presented to a senior researcher.
(C) It is the highest honor in the DuPont.
(D) It is only awarded once per decade.

185. What is suggested about the Conference on Natural History?
D
(A) It is one of several held by the AIA. *開放給大眾*
(B) It is open to the public.
(C) It is free for university researchers. *大學研究者免費*
(D) It is held in a different location each year. *每年在不同地方舉行*

文章, 資訊, 和表格

[handwritten note: Levinson財務公司要搬家]

Monday, June 23

Levinson Financial Offices to Be Relocated

[handwritten: lease v. 出租 lease out / 租凭 lease from]

YOUR AD HERE!
Call us to
advertise in
Business Daily

NEW YORK
WORLD'S FAIR
TOURS

[handwritten: n. 租約]
↳ The lease on this house expires at the end of the year. 這個房子的租約今年到期。

NEW YORK—Levinson Financial of New York State will soon be moving its <u>personnel</u> in Rochester, Syracuse, and Buffalo into company-owned buildings. The high cost of <u>leasing</u> office space <u>prompted</u> the company's decision to build. "After renting for ten years, we realized that <u>ownership</u> would <u>result in</u> significant savings," said Jamie Frazier, Levinson Financial managing director. She also noted that sharing space with other firms had become increasingly untenable. Construction of the Rochester <u>facility</u>, which began a year ago, was finished earlier this month. Employees will likely move in as soon as August.

Construction of the other two facilities, in Syracuse and Buffalo, began in February and is <u>expected to</u> <u>wrap up</u> within the next few months. The company says that its entire staff will relocate to one of the new buildings by November <u>at the latest.</u>

[handwritten notes:]
ni 員工
把員工搬進公司的大樓
租辦公室的高成本讓公司想自己蓋
租了10年之後
發現有自己的大樓可以帶來非常大的節省
所有權 導致
她也提到了和其他公司分享空間
變得越來越難以忍受的(不行的)
建設
Rochester辦公室的工程一年前開始, 這個月稍早完成了. 員工很可能搬進去不遲於8月
另外兩個地方的工程, 2月開始, 預計在接下來幾個月之內完成。
預計 完成
全部的員工
最遲

* facility 場所, 設備, 廁所, 能力
He has great facility in learning language. 他很有學習語言的才能

*prompt v. 促使, 激起
　　n. 催促, 提醒, 提示 He had to be given a prompt. 他需要被提詞
　adj. 即時的, 迅速的: He is prompt in paying his rent. 付房租都不拖的
　adv. 準時地(正): They started at 6:00 prompt. 6點整開始

GO ON TO THE NEXT PAGE.

Aladdin 公司讓搬家這件事更簡單. 從開始到結束

Aladdin makes moving easier from start to finish!

我們對於費用很誠貞的(坦率的,正當的) 搬家顧問會到你公司去做個調查

We are honest about costs. A relocation <u>consultant</u> will visit your site to

就此 adv.

complete a <u>visual</u> survey of the items to be moved. We will provide   提供

a written <u>estimate</u> within 2 days of the visit. We work with you   管理   顧問

公司拜訪後2天之內會提供   throughout the move.   management consultant 業務

予估估價單. 整個搬家的過程我們都會和您們一起。 chainsaw   "   裁員 "

■ Do you need help <u>packaging</u>? Our crew will assist you with anything

包裝   我們工作人員會協助你所有事從傢俱到

from furniture to computer systems and general equipment.

電腦系統到一般設備(一般用具)

你要搬敏感的(機要的)文件或檔案嗎?

■ Are you moving <u>sensitive</u> documents and files? With your security staff,

確保   adj.連續的

we can create a schedule to <u>ensure</u> <u>continuous</u> monitoring of

有了保全人員.我們可以用一個   <u>confidential</u> material.   *a confidential secretary*

行程表確保持續的監視   trust adj.獲信任的.機密的   機要秘書

對機密素材(文件)

■ Do you need **storage** space? We can hold your belongings at our secure,

你需要儲存空間嗎?   我們可以保存你的東西在我們安全的

climate-controlled warehouse until your new space is ready.

有空調的   倉庫   直到你的新空間準備好之後

We get the job done right. The move isn't finished until every crate is

unpacked, every item placed, every piece of <u>debris</u> <u>discarded.</u>

瓦礫   o I   a   *discard*

我們把工作做好.搬運工作不會結束直到 垃圾   *strictly*   v.拋棄丟棄

每個箱子都被打開.每個商品都被擺好   *highly confidential*

每個垃圾都被丟掉。   高度機密

＊estimate

v.估計 + for   成本估計是3百萬元   *confidentially*

+ at the cost was estimated at 3 million adv.私下地

n.估算 = a rough estimate 粗略的   dollars.   偷偷地

an accurate estimate 正確的

Please complete the request below to schedule an <u>on-site</u> cost estimate.

Company name:	Levinson Financial NY
Name of contact person:	Lane Rowley
Telephone:	210-888-4343
E-mail:	land_d@levinson.com
Pick-up address:	128 Forbes Lane, Rochester
Delivery address:	548 Village Gate Road, Rochester
Pick-up date:	August 10
Delivery date:	August 10
Preferred visual survey date and time:	August 1, between 9:00 AM and 5:00 PM

186. In the article, paragraph 1, line 5, the word "prompted" is the closest in meaning to
(A) initiated.
(B) acted quickly.
(C) made different.
(D) reminded.

187. What is implied about Ms. Frazier?
(A) She works in the Levinson Financial Syracuse office.
(B) She was promoted to managing director last year.
(C) She has been employed by Levinson Financial for 10 years.
(D) She will move to a new office by November.

188. What service does Aladdin offer?
(A) Building construction.
(B) Corporate catering.
(C) Transfer of sensitive material.
(D) Management of computer systems.

189. What is implied about the Village Gate Road Location?
(A) It was constructed in about one year.
(B) It has recently been <u>vacated</u>.
(C) It is partially leased to other companies.
(D) It will hold 500 employees.

190. What will most likely happen on August 1?
(A) Mr. Rowley will receive a written estimate.
(B) Furniture crates will be unpacked.
(C) Equipment will be removed from storage.
(D) An Aladdin employee will visit the Forbes Lane location.

GO ON TO THE NEXT PAGE.

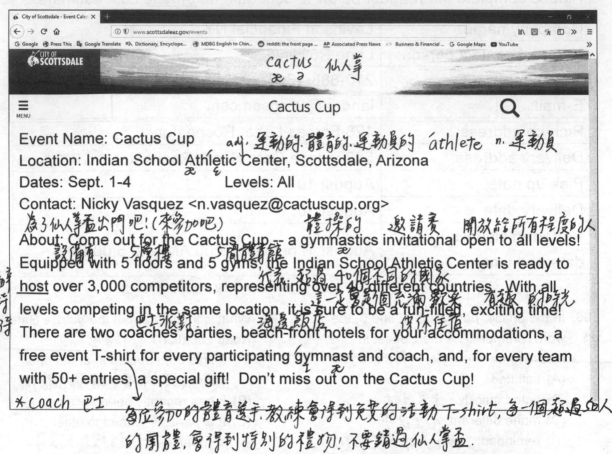

cactus 仙人掌

City of Scottsdale - Event Calen
www.scottsdaleaz.gov/events
G Google 🔗 Press This 🔗 Google Translate 🔗 Dictionary, Encyclope... 🔗 MDBG English to Chin... 🔗 reddit: the front page ... AP Associated Press News 🔗 Business & Financial ... G Google Maps ▶ YouTube

CITY OF SCOTTSDALE

≡ MENU

Cactus Cup 🔍

Event Name: Cactus Cup
adj. 運動的·體育的·運動員的 athlete *n. 運動員*

Location: Indian School Athletic Center, Scottsdale, Arizona

Dates: Sept. 1-4   Levels: All

Contact: Nicky Vasquez <n.vasquez@cactuscup.org>

為了仙人掌盃出門吧！(來參加吧)   體操的   邀請賽   開放給所有程度的人

About: Come out for the Cactus Cup -- a gymnastics invitational open to all levels!

配備有   5層樓   5間體育館   比賽 超過 40個不同的國家

Equipped with 5 floors and 5 gyms, the Indian School Athletic Center is ready to

主持   招待
host over 3,000 competitors, representing over 40 different countries. With all

                                     這一定會是個充滿驚喜 有趣 刺激的時光
levels competing in the same location, it is sure to be a fun-filled, exciting time!

           巴士派對   海景飯店   免休住宿
There are two coaches' parties, beach-front hotels for your accommodations, a

free event T-shirt for every participating gymnast and coach, and, for every team

with 50+ entries, a special gift! Don't miss out on the Cactus Cup!

*coach 巴士

每位參加的體育選手·教練會得到免費的活動 T-shirt，每一個超過50人
的團體，會得到特別的禮物! 不要錯過仙人掌盃.

SPECIALIZED
CACTUS CUP

EVENT INFO   EVENTS ▾   REGISTER   STORE

男子全能比賽結果
MEN'S ALL-AROUND RESULTS

第一名
First Place — Richard Finn, Canada 9.875

第二名
Second Place — Bernard Merkel, Germany 9.852

第三名
Third Place — Takashi Edo, Japan 9.770

第四名
Fourth Place — Keith Lubbock, Australia 9.633

第五名
Fifth Place — Jimmy Gill, U.S. 9.599

What's new in Scottsdale?

The annual Cactus Cup Gymnastics Invitational took place last weekend and it was a blockbuster success! Because of the participation of elite competitors, the number of visitors was double that of previous years. The contest drew athletes for both the solo and team categories. G-Force Acrobatic of San Diego, California, won its third straight team title. All of the events were highly competitive, featuring wonderful feats of athleticism, but by far the most exciting event was the Men's All-Around. Richard Finn from Canada beat two-time champion Bernard Merkel from Germany, with two perfect 10 scores on the high bar and rings, respectively. All the athletes were amazing but my personal favorite was Takashi Edo, a Japanese phenomenon on the parallel bars. His double-backward somersault dismount was something no one had ever seen before. Spectators could join the fun, too. Gymnasts who were not competing led a community course on floor exercise. This, along with music and vendors, provided the perfect way to enjoy the last weekend of the summer.

By Dwayne Mustaine

191. What is indicated about contestants?
(A) They are all amateurs.
(B) They are from a variety of countries.
(C) They are acquainted with Ms. Vasquez.
(D) They are requested to register in advance.

192. What is indicated about this year's event?
(A) It was held in Scottsdale for the first time.
(B) It was better attended than last year's event.
(C) It had more than 10,000 visitors.
(D) It cost $5 per person to attend.

193. In the article, the word "drew" in the paragraph 2, line 1, is closest in meaning to
(A) moved.
(B) attracted.
(C) won.
(D) pictured.

194. What is stated about Mr. Merkel?
(A) He fell on a dismount.
(B) He recently moved to Canada.
(C) He won the competition previously.
(D) He has given gymnastics lessons.

195. Whose performance did Mr. Mustaine like the most?
(A) Finn's.
(B) Edo's.
(C) Lubbock's.
(D) Gill's.

GO ON TO THE NEXT PAGE

Soho飯店系列有新老闆了
Soho Hotels Get New Owner

以倫敦為基地的Staybridge 飯店集團 收購了 Soho有限責任公司

Soho是一間規模不太大但是強調當地經營的連鎖飯店
DES MOINES (July) — The London-based Staybridge Hotel Group has
adj.排外的,獨有的,高級的 v.給予經營
acquired Soho, Inc., a small but <u>exclusive</u> locally <u>franchised</u> hotel chain.

With the addition of the Soho properties, Staybridge now operates 11 hotels

in the Des Moines area with more than 800 guest rooms.

加上 Soho 的增建物財產(飯店) Staybridge集團經營11間飯店在DM區域共超過800間客房。

收購之前 Prior to the acquisition, Staybridge had been best known for its Staybridge
Staybridge最有名的就是摘攻氣房,小飯店設計給
Regency Suites, smaller hotels designed with business travelers in mind.
商務旅行者。
Soho's four properties include the luxurious Lancaster, built in 1903, and
高檔的
The Grand Court, a <u>high-end</u> hotel that opened just last year.
Soho的四間飯店.包含豪華的Lancaster, 1903年建造
還有高端的 Grand Court, 去年開幕的 這兩間是Soho的

The Soho hotels are a very welcome addition to the Staybridge Brand,
堅固的名聲
said Staybridge spokesperson Blake Tyler. Soho has a <u>solid reputation</u> in (好名聲)

Des Moines, and with <u>accommodations</u> that <u>appeal</u> especially <u>to</u> tourists,
n.補充物.補足物
they are a perfect <u>complement</u> to Staybridge's existing hotels.

Staybridge loyalty-club members can now earn points when they stay at

any of the former Soho Hotels.
Staybridge 忠誠會員現在入住任何之前屬於Soho集團(就是被收購)皆可獲得點數

＊前頁補充　　　　　　　　　　　＊ merge 併　merger 合併
acrobatic adj.特技的　　　　　 acquire 購　acquisition 收購
high | go
'acrobat n.雜技演員.賣藝者　　Soho 對 Staybridge 來說是非常
　　　　　　　　　　　　　　　受歡迎的增加(多的飯店)
acrobatics n.特技,熟練的技巧　Soho 在 Des Moines 區有好的名聲,
　　　　　　　　　　　　　　　住宿特別吸引遊客,
　　　　　　　　　　　　　　　是Staybridge現有飯店非常好的補充

Welcome to Des Moines! Want to be in the heart of the city center? Choose Staybridge Hotel Group. Our hotel family now includes the popular Soho Hotels. Below are a few of our most popular hotels in the downtown area.

The Lancaster — Featuring complimentary wireless Internet service, deluxe bed, large screen TVs and an indoor swimming pool, this hotel is located in one of the Twin Cities most historic buildings!

The Grand Court — Grand does not begin to describe this hotel! Enjoy our newly refurbished luxurious guest rooms, fine dining at our recently remodeled restaurant, and convenient access to theaters, shopping and sightseeing.

Hotel Hennepin — With free transportation to the airport and a fully equipped business center, this is the perfect hotel for working while traveling. Featuring conference rooms and complimentary wireless Internet service, this hotel makes it easy for business travelers.

Bankside Des Moines — An old-fashioned inn with modern conveniences such as microwaves, flat-screen TVs, and refrigerators in every room. With its charming décor, tasty complimentary breakfast, and proximity to sightseeing destinations, this is a wonderful place to stay during your Des Moines holiday.

Or choose one of our many other hotels in the Des Moines region. When you choose Staybridge, you choose the best!

GO ON TO THE NEXT PAGE

43

Tripguru hotel ratings for Bankside Des Moines

Overall rating: ⊙⊙ ●●●◑○ Based on **534** traveller reviews

Most recent traveller reviews:

Cheskya Robelsk
Kiev, Ukraine

Overall Rating
●●●○○

My recent stay at the Bankside was <u>decent</u>. My room
was comfortable and <u>well furnished</u>, and all my meals
at the hotel restaurant were tasty and <u>not overpriced</u>.
The hotel staff provided <u>adequate</u> service as well.
However, I wish there had been an airport <u>shuttle
service</u>. I had a difficult time getting a taxi, and it was
expensive. <u>Aside from</u> that <u>minor inconvenience</u>, I
enjoyed my stay. <u>Three out of five stars</u>.

annotations: ※ minor 輕小的·次要的 ↔ major 重要的
整修得很好, /dɪsŋt/ 正派的·體面的·不錯的
沒有太貴
'adequate adj. 能滿足需要的 足夠的
希望能有機場接 致服務
少了很不方便
很難叫計程車·也很貴 5顆星打3顆
根據前文說 Staybridge 更吸引 商務人士和 Lancaster, Grand 去掉沒 選到 (C)

See rooms & rates

---

196. What does the article suggest about
Staybridge Hotel Chains?
(A) It <u>specializes in</u> budget hotels.
(B) It wants to appeal to a wider
variety of customers.
(C) It is relocating its headquarters.
(D) It has discontinued its rewards
program.

文章指出關於飯店的敘述何者為真？ B
專攻廉價飯店
吸引更多元的 客戶
總部要搬家
積點回饋活動停止·中斷

197. What is indicated about the four
hotels mentioned in the
advertisement?
(A) They have business centers.
(B) They were first built in 1920.
(C) They are located in downtown
Des Moines.
(D) They offer discounts to
business travelers.

C 廣告提到的四間飯店 敘述何者為真
有商務中心
1920年蓋的
在 DM 的市中心
商務旅行者 有折扣

198. Which hotel is most likely not a Soho
Property?
(A) The Lancaster.
(B) The Grand Court.
(C) Hotel Hennepin.
(D) Bankside Des Moines.

哪一間最可能不是 Soho 的飯店？ C

199. What information is provided about the
hotel in which Ms. Robelsk has stayed?
(A) Its restaurant has been updated.
(B) It provides free breakfast.
(C) It is available for conferences.
(D) It includes a gift shop.

Bankside Des Moines Hotel
B
可以開會
有禮品店

200. What disappointed Ms. Robelsk about
her stay?
(A) The low quality of the restaurant.
(B) The lack of affordable transportation.
(C) The unfriendly staff.
(D) The high price of the room.

B 餐廳的低品質
不和善的員工
房間價高
缺少可負擔 的交通

Stop! This is the end of the test. If you finish before time is called, you may go
back to Parts 5, 6, and 7 and check your work.

New TOEIC Speaking Test

Question 1: Read a Text Aloud

5 Question 1

Directions: In this part of the test, you will read aloud the text on the screen.
You will have 45 seconds to prepare. Then you will have 45
seconds to read the text aloud.

不像公司聘請的代理人，獨立保險代理人和保險經紀人代表超過
Unlike company-employed agents, independent insurance agents
一間的保險公司
and insurance brokers represent more than one insurance company,
所以他們可以提供客戶更廣泛的選擇. 在車子,居家,生意,生活
so they can offer clients a wider choice of auto, home, business, life,
還有健康保障 和退休私員工福利商品
and health coverage as well as retirement and employee-benefit
獨立的代理人和經紀人不只建議客戶關於保險的事
products. Independent agents and brokers not only advise clients
他們也推廣損害防阻的想法可以減少損失
about insurance. They also recommend loss-prevention ideas that
如果損失發生　　　獨立的保險經紀人或代理人
can cut costs. If a loss occurs, the independent insurance agent or
和客戶同一陣線直到索賠完成
broker stands with the client until the claim is settled.

＊claim n. 索賠,要求,主張
ie,
v. ＇, ＇, 聲稱,需要：The trend claims our attention.
(疾病,意外)奪去生命：The tornado claimed dozens of lives.

PREPARATION TIME	dozens of 幾10條
00 : 00 : 45	a dozen of 10幾

20 something 20幾
→ There are twenty something
students in the classroom.

RESPONSE TIME
00 : 00 : 45

GO ON TO THE NEXT PAGE

Question 2: Read a Text Aloud

Directions: In this part of the test, you will read aloud the text on the screen. You will have 45 seconds to prepare. Then you will have 45 seconds to read the text aloud.

幾年以前，我們公司必須決定要不要撤到郊區，比較不貴，而且

A few years ago, our company had to decide whether or not we

wanted to move to the suburbs, where it would be less expensive and

拓展比較容易的地方。或是依然停在我們長期的駐地西雅圖市區。The

easier to expand, or stay in our long-time home, urban Seattle. The

答案蠻明顯的，我們決定待在城市裡有好多的原因。

answer was quite obvious—we decided to stay in the city for a

由於種種原因　我們為何要擇留在西雅圖其中一個我最愛

multitude of reasons. One of my favorite reasons why we chose to

的原因是因為我們想和這個充滿生氣，成長當中

stay in Seattle is because we want to be connected to this vibrant,

的社會有聯結。　留在這個城市也提供了我們強化和一些非營利鄰立

growing community. Staying in the city also affords us the opportunity

合夥的機會。

to strengthen our partnerships with some of our nonprofit neighbors.

城市的　⟷　鄉村的

urban　　　　rural

metropolitan　　'rustic　The village has a certain rustic

　　　　　　　^　　charm.

這個村莊有種賢樸的美(魅力)

urban dweller 城市居民　　　afford + to V 買得起

'vibrant adj. 活潑的　　　　　有足夠的... 去做...
红　振動的
　　充滿生氣的

PREPARATION TIME
00 : 00 : 45

RESPONSE TIME
00 : 00 : 45

Question 3: Describe a Picture

Directions: In this part of the test, you will describe the picture on your screen in as much detail as you can. You will have 30 seconds to prepare your response. Then you will have 45 seconds to speak about the picture.

PREPARATION TIME

00 : 00 : 30

RESPONSE TIME

00 : 00 : 45

GO ON TO THE NEXT PAGE

Question 3: Describe a Picture

答題範例

🎧 **6** **Question 3**

cleaning n. 打掃.去汙.清洗

人在一間清洗店。
The people are in a cleaning shop.

很有可能   這間店很有可能是乾洗店
The business is <u>most likely</u> a dry cleaners.

The shop offers professional cleaning of clothing.
這間店提供專業衣服清洗

There are three people in the frame. 有3個人在圖片框框中

One woman is a customer. 有個女人是客人

She <u>appears to be</u> paying for some services.
她似乎要為一些服務付費 appear to V. 似乎.看起來好像

Another woman is at the cash register. 另外一個女人在收銀台

She has very large earrings. 她有非常大的耳環

She's also wearing a baseball cap. 她巴戴著頂棒球帽。

第三個女人在遠遠的木櫃台那邊
The third woman is over by the far counter.   obscure   v.使變暗
她被一個大的金屬掛架遮住了   /əbˈskjur/   遮掩
She's obscured by a large metal hanging rack.   混淆

She's most likely preparing clothes that have been cleaned.
她很有可能在準備已經清理好的衣物

There are several racks in the background. 背景有好幾個架子

Most of them contain clean clothing. 大部份的架子有包含(有掛)

The clothes are wrapped in plastic.   乾淨衣服
衣服用塑膠包起來
→客人面前的木櫃台有些衣服
There are clothes on the counter in front of the customer.

A sign in the background advertises a particular service.   背景有塊牌子
廣告拜珠服務
The customer has her back to the camera.
顧客便她的背對著鏡頭(她背對鏡頭)

72

Questions 4-6: Respond to Questions

 **Question 4**

Directions: In this part of the test, you will answer three questions. For each question, begin responding immediately after you hear a beep. No preparation time is provided. You will have 15 seconds to respond to Questions 4 and 5 and 30 seconds to respond to Question 6.

Imagine that you are talking to a friend on the telephone.

Question 4
What did you do last weekend and with whom did you do it?

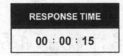

Question 5
What do you have planned this weekend?

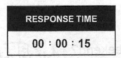

Question 6
My cousins are coming to visit this weekend, but I haven't made any plans. What do you suggest I do with them?

GO ON TO THE NEXT PAGE

Questions 4-6: Respond to Questions

How was your weekend? 答題範例

問的是週末的心情

不是做了什麼事.

🎧 6 Question 4

What did you do last weekend and with whom did you do it?

上週末你做了什麼和誰一起?

Answer

我和一些朋友去露營

I went camping with some friends.

The campsite is up north in the woods. 營區在森林的
上面靠北的地方

We spent two nights in a log cabin.

我們有二個晚上住在小木屋裡

log n. 原木; (飛行.航海) 日誌

cabin n. 客艙

🎧 6 Question 5

What do you have planned this weekend? 你這週末的計劃是什麼?

Answer

Nothing special. 沒啥特別的.

I'm going to take it easy. 我要輕鬆面對 (不安排)

I'm tired from last weekend. 我上週太累了. (從上週累到)
現在

74

《《 6 》》 **Question 6**

我的表(兄弟姐妹)這週末要來,但是我還沒有任何計劃

My cousins are coming to visit this weekend, but I haven't made any plans.

What do you suggest I do with them? 你建議我帶他們去做什麼?

Answer

那~你可以帶他們去夜市開始

Well, you could start with a visit to a night market.

夜市好玩也有趣

The night market is fun and interesting.

你的表(兄弟姐妹)可能會喜歡。

Your cousins might enjoy that.

(D) Cool beans 好吧!
Let's go to the movies.
Cool beans!

在象山有音樂會。

There's also a music festival on Elephant Mountain.

週五開始一直到週之

It starts on Friday afternoon and runs through Sunday.

If they like music, that would be (cool)

如果他們喜歡音樂,那會很棒的.

You should consider going on a hike. 你可以考慮去健行

There are many great hiking trails around the city. 城市附近有很多

That way, your cousins can appreciate some of the local 不錯的健行步道。

natural beauty. 這樣一來,他們可以欣賞到一些

當地的自然美.

*appreciate v. 欣賞. 感謝. 感激

GO ON TO THE NEXT PAGE.

food stamp 糧票
→ a government-issued coupon that is sold at little cost or given to low-income persons and is redeemable for food

((5)) **Question 7**

Directions: In this part of the test, you will answer three questions based on the information provided. You will have 30 seconds to read the information before the questions begin. For each question, begin responding immediately after you hear a beep. No additional preparation time is provided. You will have 15 seconds to respond to Questions 7 and 8 and 30 seconds to respond to Question 9.

parkade
n. 多層停車場   *哥倫比亞農夫市集*

Columbia Farmers Market

When: March 17 (8:00 am – 12:00 pm)
Where: Parkade Center, Northeast Parking Lot C
Contact: Corrina Smith
Phone: 573-823-6889   *來我們農夫市集感受一下Missouri中部的味道吧!*
Website: http://www.columbiafarmersmarket.org   *org = organization*

Experience the taste of mid-Missouri at the Columbia Farmers Market! Find us every Saturday from 8 am to noon (mid-March–mid-November) in our new temporary location, the northeast Parkade Center's parking lot (601 Business Loop 70W). *暫時的地點*

工匠, 技工   *身勞製造(生產者)可以加入的市集*

Fresh vegetables & fruit, meat, farm fresh eggs, cheeses, honey, cut flowers, plants, artisan items & more. (As) a producer-only market, everything sold here is offered by the farmers and artisans who help *好撐* sustain our region. SNAP (food stamps) accepted at all markets. Live *承擔* music every Saturday! Rain or Shine! (up)

破土   *發生*
Groundbreaking should take place this spring at the Clary-Shy Agriculture Park. While construction takes place, we will be setting up in the northeast lot at Parkade Center. Make sure to follow our social media pages to stay up-to-date on the progress.
社群媒體   了解最新的動向

Hi, I'm interested in the Farmers Market. Would you mind if I asked a few questions?

PREPARATION TIME
00 : 00 : 30

Question 7	Question 8	Question 9
RESPONSE TIME	RESPONSE TIME	RESPONSE TIME
00 : 00 : 15	00 : 00 : 15	00 : 00 : 30

Questions 7-9: Respond to Questions Using Information Provided

答題範例

《6》 **Question 7**

這個活動何時, 何地舉行?

When and where does the event take place?

Answer

農夫市集每個週又都有

The Farmers Market takes place every Saturday.

8點開始, 大約中午結束

It starts at 8:00 AM and ends around noon.

在東北方C停車場舉辦

It's held in the Northeast Parking Lot C of Parkade Center.

多層停車場中心的

《6》 **Question 8**

市集總是在這個地點舉行嗎?

Is the market always held in this location?

臨時的, 暫時的   永恆的
temporary ←→ permanent
ㄢ   ㄗㄜㄙ
momentary   lasting
Short-lived   eternal

Answer

No. 不是的

The northeast Parkade Center's parking lot is a temporary

location. 這又是個暫時的地點

Our permanent spot at the Clary-Shy Agriculture Park will
     ㄙ ㄉ ㄛ
open this spring. 我們永久的地點在 Clary-Shy

將會在春天開幕。

GO ON TO THE NEXT PAGE→

Questions 7-9: Respond to Questions Using Information Provided

《 6 》 **Question 9**

ι 期待. 預期

What can I <u>expect</u> to find at the market, or, is there anything else I should

know? 我在市集裡可以找到什麼? 或者有任何事是我應該知道

的嗎?

Answer

嗯, 首先　　每樣市集裡賣的商品都是從當地生產者(農夫)

Well, first of all, everything sold at the market is from a

local producer or artisan. 或是工匠來的。

So, these are the same people that help sustain our

region. 所以, 這些和幫維護區域發展的是同一批人

The market is a celebration of their bounty. ＊bounty

這個市集是他們收成的慶典 n.收成

你會找到農場般新鮮的水果和蔬菜 捕獲

You'll find farm-fresh fruit and vegetables. 獎金

你會發現蜂蜜和起司 大方

You'll find honey and cheese.

你也會找到手工的工匠商品 →He is famous for

You'll also find hand-crafted artisan products. his bounty to the poor.

最後, 你會找到花和植物

Finally, you'll find flowers and plants. 他因對窮人大方而出名

我們也有現場樂團

We also have a live band.

我們也接受糧票

We accept food stamps, too.

Question 10: Propose a Solution

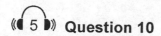 **Question 10**

Directions: In this part of the test, you will be presented with a problem and asked to propose a solution. You will have 30 seconds to prepare. Then you will have 60 seconds to speak. In your response, be sure to show that you recognize the problem, and propose a way of dealing with the problem.

In your response, be sure to

- show that you recognize the caller's problem, and
- propose a way of dealing with the problem.

PREPARATION TIME
00 : 00 : 30

RESPONSE TIME
00 : 01 : 00

GO ON TO THE NEXT PAGE

Question 10: Propose a Solution

答題範例

Voice Message

嗨 Derek, 我是人力資源部門的 Grace Peterson.
Hello, Derek? It's Grace Peterson calling from Human

我知道我們安排了明天下午見面
Resources. I know we're scheduled to meet tomorrow

看一下修正過後的兼職員工保險計畫
afternoon to go over the revised insurance plans for

但是我不能到了　　　　　　一些
part-time employees, but I won't be able to make it. Some

新的雇員明天開始上班, 我被要求帶他們看看這棟大樓
new hires are starting tomorrow, and I was asked to show

修正版本現在已完成, 所有的條例
them around the building. The revisions are now complete

都符合指導方針　　　　既然我知道你在等
and all plans fall within the guidelines. Since I know you're

這份資訊, 你介不介意請 Richard 告訴你相關資訊
waiting on this information, do you mind asking Richard to

他和我一樣熟悉這個計畫.
fill you in? He's just as familiar with the plan as I am, <u>if</u>

<u>not more so.</u> 就算沒比我熟, 至少我一樣熟

Writing is as useful as reading, if not more so.
寫作和閱讀一樣有用, 就算不比 reading 更有用, 也一樣有用。

Question 10: Propose a Solution

答題範例

我收到你的訊息了
Hi Grace, I got your message.

我明白你不能參加明天的會議
I understand that you cannot attend the meeting tomorrow.

I heard that we have some new hires coming on board. 我聽說我們
有新雇員要來上班了。

The revisions are indeed important. 修正版的確很重要

I'll need them to balance the budget. 我需要它們來平衡預算

The sooner I get them, the better. 我越早拿到越好

× contact with
✓ contact

I'll try to <u>get a hold of</u> Richard. 我會聯絡 Richard.

He's been busy lately and hasn't returned my calls. 他最近很忙,
還沒回我電話

Would you remind him to contact me?
你會提醒他聯絡我嗎?

Meanwhile, I have another idea. 同時,我有另外的想法

Why don't you e-mail me the revisions? 你為什麼不郵寄修正版
電 給我呢?
That way, we can eliminate one step of the process.
這樣一來,我們可以排除這個流程中的一個步驟

I don't think it will be necessary for Richard to fill me in. 我覺得不一定要

I'm familiar with the plans. 我對這方案也很熟悉   Richard 跟我解釋

So, I think that would be the best course of action.
我覺得這會是這個行動(拿 revision)最好的過程

I'll look for your e-mail. 我會期待你的郵件

Thanks for your help.

Have a great tomorrow. 祝明天順利。

GO ON TO THE NEXT PAGE

Question 11: Express an Opinion

((● 5 ●)) Question 11

Directions: In this part of the test, you will give your opinion about a specific topic. Be sure to say as much as you can in the time allowed. You will have 15 seconds to prepare. Then you will have 60 seconds to speak.

普遍而言，人們現在活得比較長，討論這個現象的原因

In general, people are living longer now. Discuss the causes of this

phenomenon. Use specific reasons and details to develop your answer.

提出明確的理由和細節去發展你的答案

（詳盡闡述）

PREPARATION TIME
00 : 00 : 15

RESPONSE TIME
00 : 01 : 00

Question 11: Express an Opinion

*nutrition n. 營養(品.學)
life adj. 生命的
     n. 生命

*expectancy n. 期待. 預期 life expectancy 壽命
答題範例 → Women have a higher life expectancy than men.

《6》 Question 11
'hygiene n. 衛生

*dissemination n. 宣傳. 傳播
[ɪ ɛ ə e]

食物. 營養. 健康和衛生

The three big reasons that people are living longer lives are: <u>food supply and nutrition</u>, <u>health</u>, and <u>hygiene</u>. 從19. 20世紀以來. 這3項的標準都有較大的改進

All three have seen major improvements in standards since the nineteenth and early twentieth centuries. 然而. 另一個重要的因素是知道這些對我們的健康和壽命長短

However, another important <u>factor</u> is knowing their importance to our health and <u>life</u> <u>expectancy</u>. 的重要性

採取一些必要的步驟. 可以保證健康的生活方式. 由於科學研究的結果

By taking necessary steps we can ensure a healthy lifestyle. 我們取得資訊也改進了

Our access to information has also improved as a result of scientific research.

adv. 戲劇性地. 誇張地

Methods of information dissemination, for example, the Internet, have increased <u>dramatically</u>.

資訊傳播的方法. 比如說網路. 大幅地增加 → 比如. 食品的包裝要標示食物的

For example, the packaging of food products must display the nutritional content of food. 成分

Some products use color-coding so that we know whether they are good for us.

The importance of eating a balanced diet is widely known. 有些食物用顏色標記. 所以我們知道

大家都知道均衡飲食的重要性 是否對我們有益處。

Government websites provide information about the lifestyle choices we can make in order to reduce our risk of developing diseases. 政府網站提供資訊關於生活模式選擇

The dangers of smoking cigarettes are included on packaging. 為了減少得病的風險。吸煙的

Smoking is banned in most public places, and the age limit has been raised to 18 years. 危險也顯示

抽煙在很多公眾場合是禁止的. 年齡限制也被提高到18歲 在包裝上

Advertisements on buses and tubes inform us of the importance of washing our hands.

There are signs reminding us to cover our mouths when we cough or sneeze. 洗手. 遮口鼻

Health and safety legislation provides strict regulations for hygiene in restaurants, hospitals and factories. 健康. 安全法規提供對於餐廳. 醫院. 工廠嚴格的衛生規定

追隨健康的生活模式是個選擇. 但並不是每個人都會這麼做. 或是都有能力這麼做

But following a healthy lifestyle is still a choice that we make, and not everyone chooses it or is able to do so. 真的的長壽現象是人們有著不好的生活模式但活到100歲

The real phenomenon of longevity is people with terrible lifestyles who live to be 100 years old. 因此. 應該有些遺傳的成分包含在其中 *involve v.包含.使捲入.牽涉. 牽累

Therefore, there must be some kind of a genetic component involved.

不能被忽視的. 接種可能比其它任何因素對壽命帶來的影響更大

Not to be overlooked, vaccinations have probably done more for life expectancy than any one factor. *[æ n ə]* 人們不再受時疫(像是小兒麻痺)滅絕

People are no longer getting wiped out by epidemics like <u>polio</u>.

In my opinion, improvements in medical care are the main reason people live so long.

就我而言. 醫療照顧的改進是人們活那麼長的主要原因

GO ON TO THE NEXT PAGE.

New TOEIC Writing Test

Questions 1-5: Write a Sentence Based on a Picture

Question 1

Directions: Write ONE sentence based on the picture using the TWO words or phrases under it. You may change the forms of the words and you may use them in any order.

woman / drive

*drive

① 駕車旅行：The woman is going for a drive.

② 宣傳活動：The manager decided to launch a sales drive.

　　　　經理決定推出一個銷售宣傳活動

③ 幹勁：He is a man of great drive.　　田啟望

答題範例：**A woman is driving a bus.**

GO ON TO THE NEXT PAGE ➞

Questions 1-5: Write a Sentence Based on a Picture

Question 2

Directions: Write ONE sentence based on the picture using the TWO words or phrases under it. You may change the forms of the words and you may use them in any order.

*de|scend ①下來、下降　**hikers / descend**
down | climb
　　　　② 傳下來: The custom has descended to our day.
　　　　　　這個習俗一直傳到今天

customs n. 海關、關稅　　costume　n. 服裝、戲服
/ˈkʌstəmz/　　　　　　/ˈkastjum/

　　The hikers walked in a line as they descended the
答題範例: **The hikers are descending a hill.**　　mountain.
　　Several hikers

86

Questions 1-5: Write a Sentence Based on a Picture

Question 3

Directions: Write ONE sentence based on the picture using the TWO words or phrases under it. You may change the forms of the words and you may use them in any order.

seat / meeting

seat
n. 座位, 職位, 所在地
→ Universities are seats of learning.
大學是學習的地方
→ 請坐. take a seat
       have a seat

① v. 使就座
→ He seated himself in a chair.
→ Please be seated. 〈正式〉
② 容納
→ The classroom seats 45 people.

答題範例: **Some men are seated for a meeting.**
Some people are in their seats and ready to start the meeting.

sit v. 只有動詞用法 (口語)
She sits between Tack and Tom.(口)   She is seated between Tack and
請坐 sit down, please.   Tom.〈正式〉

GO ON TO THE NEXT PAGE.

Questions 1-5: Write a Sentence Based on a Picture

Question 4

Directions: Write ONE sentence based on the picture using the TWO words or phrases under it. You may change the forms of the words and you may use them in any order.

* It rained off and on all　**road / truck**
斷斷續續地下了一天雨　day.

We don't go there regularly, just off and on. 沒有經常去. 偶爾去一次

There are several trucks both <u>on and off</u> the road.
The tow truck is removing the minivan from the road.

答題範例：**There are several trucks on the side of the road.**

88

Questions 1-5: Write a Sentence Based on a Picture

Question 5

Directions: Write ONE sentence based on the picture using the TWO words or phrases under it. You may change the forms of the words and you may use them in any order.

men / sign

The men are posing for a picture with a sign.
Only one man is on the left side of the sign.
*sign ① 標誌，招牌: The sign says no parking. ③ 薪水
② 手勢，暗示: I talked with him by signs. 我和他用手勢交談

答題範例：**Three men are standing next to a sign.**

GO ON TO THE NEXT PAGE.

Questions 6-7: Respond to a written request

Question 6

Directions: Read the e-mail below.

*inquire about 詢問
for 求見
into 調查
after 問候

*conflict n. 衝突、v. conflict 衝突
*slot n. 狹縫、行程表中一格

From: Rondell Clayburn	
To: Rebecca Christiansen	
Re: Program change	
Sent: July 16	

我很期待在兩天之後與您在第8屆國際貿易年度國際會議見面。

Dear Ms. Christiansen,

I am looking forward to meeting you at the 8th Annual International Conference on International Trade in just two short days!

你詢問過關於有沒有可能把你的演講移到比較早的時間搭程

You had inquired about the possibility of moving your talk to an earlier

我們剛剛有個取消

time slot. We have just had a cancellation. Moira Brown has a

有行程衝突　　而且要我把她的演說改晚一點

scheduling conflict and has requested to give her talk later in the day.

因此　　　　10:30那格時間是可以的　　　　有你的同意

Therefore, her 10:30 slot on Day 1 is available. With your approval, I

我想把你的演說移到那個

would like to move your talk to that time.

我需要知道你是否會使用到會議中心提供的電腦、或是　　　時候

I need to know whether you will be using the computer provided by

是否需連接你自己的電腦到投影機

the conference center or whether you will need to connect your own

還有 你演講時需要用到網路嗎？

computer to the projector. Also, will you require Internet access during

要、需、命令

your talk? Please let me know at your earliest convenience.

一有空就告訴我

Sincerely yours,

Rondell Clayburn

Chairman, Organizing Committee

8th Annual International Conference on International Trade

以Christiansen的身份

回信給Clayburn、同意改時間、和回答他的兩個問題

Directions: Write back to Mr. Clayburn as Ms. Christiansen. AGREE to the time change and answer BOTH of his questions.

答題範例

＊ according to 根據 (把所根據的事物放後面當 O.)

Question 6→ Please park your car according to the instruction.

accordingly 按照已捉之條件做出反應

Mr. Clayburn, Please see to the instruction and park your car

謝你的訊息，我也很期待在會議上跟你見面　accordingly.

Thank you for your message, and I'm looking forward to meeting you at the

關於　　　提議的　行程改變

conference as well. In regards to the proposed program change, 10:30 on

Day 1 would work perfectly for me. I approve the change and will plan to

我同意以時間，我同意這項改變，也會依照相對應

appear accordingly. (wp)

相應地　的討論出席 　→我會帶自己的電腦，而且沒錯，

I will be bringing my own computer, and yes, Internet access would be

連線電腦是非常感謝的。(很需要)　我也會帶自己的 Wi-Fi 熱點.

greatly appreciated. I will also bring my own Wi-Fi hotspot, just in case.

以防萬一

Again, thank you and I'll see you on Friday.

＊ remedy – remedied – remedied 藥重藥物

Sincerely,　　　　　　治療

Rebecca Christiansen　　If I made a mistake,

I'll try to remedy it.

各種治療

Aspirin may remedy a stomachache.

＊ cure – cured – cured 治病

The doctor cured her of a cold.　　＊ treat – treated – treated 診治病人

The medicine will cure your headache.　The dentist is treating my teeth.

She was cured of her disease.　　The doctor is not able to treat this

disease.

＊ heal – healed – healed 治癒傷口

Time heals all broken hearts.

The sergeon healed the soldier's bullet wound in the leg.

外科醫師治療了軍人的子彈傷口

腳上

GO ON TO THE NEXT PAGE

Questions 6-7: Respond to a written request

Question 7

Directions: Read the e-mail below.

From: Mark Clark	ask a favor of you 請你幫忙
To: Sally Kimmock	Could you do me a favor?
Date: Thursday, July 23	give me a hand?
Subject: Job Reference	* culinary adj.烹飪的.廚房的

Dear Ms. Kimmock,

身為你們烹飪學校的前學員,我需要請你幫個忙。

As one of your former students at Crestford Academy of Culinary Arts, I need

我畢業在巴爾的摩的The Oceanaire海鮮餐廳中找工作

to ask a favor of you. I am applying for a position at The Oceanaire Seafood

想知道我是否可以用你們當備查資料

Room in Baltimore and would like to know if I may use you as a reference since

因為你們的課和這份工作最相關   請你有空便回覆

your class was most relevant to the job. Please let me know at your earliest

我這周末要繳交我的申請表,而且要附上

convenience. I would like to submit my application by the end of this week and

我的資料在線上申請表上。   我有附加文件

need to include my references in the online application. I have attached a

讓你審查   包含了工作描述和我的履歷

document for you to review. It includes both the job description and my resume.

再次謝謝你的指導.   我很開心上你的課

Thank you again for your instruction. I enjoyed being in your class.

*reference

Mark Clark n.推薦信、備查資料.(佐證曾在那裡上班/b課過)

參考文獻

'kjulɪ,nɛrɪ/ + workers 廚房的工人
+ skills 烹調技術

Directions: Reply as Sally Kimmock and AGREE to Mark Clark's request.

Give ONE reason why he would be a good candidate for the

job, and ONE suggestion about his application and resume.

給出一個理由.告訴他為何他是這個工作的好候選人
關於他的履歷和申請表給出一個建議

Questions 6-7: Respond to a written request

答題範例

Question 7

Mark,

我很榮幸能當你的推薦資料　你擷起（聲）課堂上
I would be happy to serve as a reference. You picked up the

的資訊非常快，　　　　　　　所以我想你會成為
information presented in our class very quickly, so I think you'll be a

一個好的適合人選，對於這個快速步調的工作環境
good fit for a fast-paced environment like The Oceanaire Seafood

我看了你的履歷，並只是想提醒你
Room. I reviewed your resume and just wanted to remind you that

這個課程是有證照的
the class was one that contributes to a certificate. You completed

你6月完成了這個課程，所以你應該指出了你淨到了
the program in June, so you should indicate that you earned a

Level 2的ACF證照
Level II ACF certification.

　　　　　* contribute v. 提供，貢獻，捐助

Best wishes!
　　　　　* certificate n. 證書，執照

Sally Kimmock

* favor n. 幫助，善意的行為，贊同
　　　　v. 支持，偏愛，偏袒

* in favor of
　　贊成 Are you in favor of the new project?
　　　　I'm all in favor of equal pay for equal work.
　　我完全贊同同工同酬

* In favor with = be popular with
　　受到～寵愛，得到～好評，重視
　　This dance is in favor with young people.

GO ON TO THE NEXT PAGE ➡

Questions 8: Write an opinion essay

Question 8

Directions: Read the question below. You have 30 minutes to plan, write, and revise your essay. Typically, an effective response will contain a minimum of 300 words.

Neighbors are the people who live near us. In your opinion, what are the qualities of a good neighbor? Use specific details and examples in your answer.

鄰居, 就是住離我們很近的人。

以你的意見, 什麼是好鄰居的條件

用詳細的細節和例子回答。

* specific

adj. 特殊的

明確的

具體的

* neighbor n. 鄰居, 鄰近的人, 鄰國

    adj. 鄰近的. 鄰接的

    v. 與~為鄰 Our school neighbors on a square.

       我們學校旁邊是個廣場

* neighborhood n. 鄰近地區, 鄰里情誼

→ They live in good neighborhood with one another.

    他們和鄰里關係10分和睦

Questions 8: Write an opinion essay

Question 8

台北是個居住密集的城市，有很多人員的住在彼此的上面，因此，幾乎所有人都住在鄰居

Taipei is a <u>densely populated</u> city with many people literally living on top of each other.

讓附近的公寓，每個方向

Therefore, almost everybody lives in an apartment with neighbors in close proximity, in

都有，上面，下面，對面，後面　　在這樣的情況之下，知道每一個好鄰居是很重要的

every direction—up, down, across, and behind. In this situation, it is important to know how

to be a good neighbor.

第一點，好鄰居要安靜　　任何曾經住在吵雜鄰居隔壁的人都可以證明這點

First of all, good neighbors are quiet. Anyone who has ever lived next to noisy

證明　　　　　　　　　　　　有見似個人住在同棟大樓

neighbors can <u>attest to this</u>. Good neighbors are aware that there are other people living

把噪音用到最小　　他們不會尖叫或是音樂開很大或是舉辦

in the building and keep noise to a minimum. They don't scream or blare music or throw

不會　到很晚　　　　　　　他們不會大力關門，也不會在走廊大叫

parties until late hours in the evening. They don't slam doors and yell in the hallways.

他們對附近的人表現出尊重

They show some respect for those around them.

尊重他們的社區　　　　　　任何把垃圾留在走廊

Next, good neighbors respect their community. Anyone who leaves garbage or junk

停車場 或是其他共同區域的人都不是好鄰居

in the hallways, in the parking lot or in other common areas is not a good neighbor. A

一個允許他把自己的垃圾堆積在公共空間的人，對不尊重且他住在這棟大樓的人

neighbor who allows his or her junk to accumulate in shared spaces shows disrespect for

好鄰居展現基本的禮貌　並且定時　把垃圾

everyone else in the building. Good neighbors show common courtesy and regularly take

倒掉 和保持公共區域乾淨

out their trash and keep shared and public areas clean.

除此之外，　好鄰居成熟的處理各種狀況　　如果一個好鄰居對某人

有疑問

Additionally, good neighbors handle situations maturely. If a good neighbor has a

比如說　有個房客的狗最近一直大聲吵

problem with someone, for example, a tenant whose dog has been barking a lot recently,

他要親切的靠近這個人說這件事　　　　同樣地，他/她考慮

he or she would kindly approach the person about the matter. Likewise, he or she takes

別人可能反對他自身行為的擔憂（別人對他有就像他也會反應）

into account the concerns of others who may object to his or her own behavior. Everyone

每個人能更好的相處，問題就比較快解決，當人們像成熟的大人看待時

gets along better and problems are solved faster when people behave like mature adults.

或是變成消極侵略的報復方法

Bad neighbors don't handle situations maturely. They ignore others, respond rudely or

turn to <u>passive aggressive retaliation</u> methods. Good neighbors never behave that way.

工作上 報復　當他們可以 呼叫幫助別人　並沒有規定說

What's more, good neighbors help when and where they can. There isn't a rule stating

好鄰居應該要伸出　　　　　　但大體而言

that good neighbors should lend a helping hand, but in general, they do. Good neighbors

借你key去樓下洗衣房當你忘記key放哪裡的時候

let you borrow a key to the downstairs laundry room when you've misplaced yours. Good

和你合作　　和房東溝通　　　　　　關於樓道的維修問題

neighbors will team up with you to speak with the landlord about a maintenance issue in

the common stairwell. <u>Ultimately</u>, they're looking to reside in a pleasant, friendly and safe

最後，好鄰居也想 ——→ 居住在一個愉快的，和善的和安全的環境

environment, too.

不論一個人的居住狀況如何，好鄰居很重要，找到好鄰居的方法就是自己成為一個好鄰居

No matter what one's living situation is, having good neighbors is important. The best

way to find good neighbors is to first be a good neighbor to others.